Faithfully Addicted

Darren Finney

5310 Publishing

FAITHFULLY
Addicted

What happens when love can't happen?

DARREN FINNEY

5310
publishing
5310 Publishing Company
5310publishing.com

SCAN ME

ISBN (paperback): 9781777151812
ISBN (ebook): 9781777151829

Author: Darren Finney
Cover design: Eric Williams - 5310 Publishing
Editor: Alex Williams – 5310 Publishing

First edition (this edition) released in June 2021.

1 | 21

Prologue

She tore the page from the notebook then threw it at the already overflowing trash bin. In the group session, they said that writing down her feelings would help her work through them and provide a tool for her to look back on and see her progress. All it was doing was testing her already nonexistent patience.

She had tried keeping it like a diary, even posting each date as she wrote before giving up feeling like she was taking observation notes on a lab rat. The last thing she had wanted to feel like right now was an experiment. That notebook was at the bottom of the trash bin too. If they had let her have a lighter or even a candle, she imagined she would have burnt it.

Picking up the pen again, she decided to try what another man in the group was doing. He had admitted to writing letters, although he would probably never let her read them. The man said that it's easier to work through what he was thinking by addressing the letters to his wife rather than keeping a journal. She had wondered if he had felt what she was calling "lab rat syndrome."

As steadily as her hand still allowed, she wrote *Dear* at the top of the page then froze. She realized she did not know who she would write these to. She did not know if she wanted someone to read them, or more importantly, that she could think of anyone right now that would read them if she did send the letters to them. She ripped the page from the notebook and sent it on a trajectory very similar to the last page.

On the next page, she wrote: *To whom it may concern,* then smiled to herself. She liked that. It was noncommittal while at the same time giving her just *someone* to tell. For the first time, she felt like she wanted to try this.

To whom it may concern,

They tell me this is supposed to help. That by writing this all down that maybe I will be able to cope. I seriously don't know if I believe that. Do you? Pray tell, do you believe that a letter into the void would lead to some deep purging of that abyss in my soul. I hope you do. I want to believe it too.

I feel so trapped. I have to wonder if this would let me be free. Not that I know what that would feel like either, but it has to feel better than this, doesn't it? Does freedom hurt? I know everyone will always say it requires sacrifice but is it worth it? I'm scared to find out.

Evermore,

She stopped realizing she had no idea how she intended to sign it. For some reason, putting her name felt like it gave these thoughts too much power. She reread the letter and realized that she had admitted more in this one short letter than she had through any of her sessions thus far. She closed the notebook, scared of what else she may admit if she wrote anymore tonight.

Faithfully Addicted

Chapter I

To whom it may concern,

What, pray tell, are you so scared of? It is, as they say, at least I suspect, that the truth will set you free. Is it that very thought that scares you? Freedom? Of all your fears, that would be the one at the forefront of everything. Freedom would terrify someone who could never understand what it meant not to be shackled to the weight always pulling them under. Freedom would paralyze someone who lived, believing that they did not need to escape. If you wonder how that is possible, just know, friend, that some prisoners don't even see the fence that they can't climb. Their perspective has become so warped that they think they are right where they need to be.

That's the sad truth, and I don't mean 'sad' as in sympathetic because I do pity you. I mean 'sad' as in pathetic because you disgust me. Perhaps because I see just a little too much of myself in you, you are that hateful reminder. We all spend so much time between being free and being a captive that most of us have gotten used to the bars. It's true, and the average person doesn't even see them anymore. Yet here you are. Locked away in some dark little cell with your face pressed to the bars on the window, afraid that maybe someday someone will decide that you have paid your time. Early release with good behavior? Let's be realistic; that's not likely, but eventually, somebody is going to find the key to your cell, and they are even going to go so far as to discover it's not empty, and the truth is that terrifies you.

For once, your reaction is not disdainful but unfortunately understandable, even if I still don't like it. It's a common thing among veterans, ex-cons, and addicts, actually — that inability to adjust to life after. The bars, the fences, the walls, and the structures of life are stripped away and called freedom, but nobody explains how to adjust to that. Then they have to watch as the life they have built falls apart all over again. They simply cannot take it. They would rather have the bars *and the chains and the structures captivity than the freewill to build their own shelter.*

So, I get it. I would even go so far as to say I understand it. The simplest truth is that you are a coward. You would rather stay locked away if there is the smallest chance you would have to stomach that particular heartbreak. You would rather not taste freedom if there is the chance that you would have to swallow that bitter pill that you do not know how to live free. Go ahead, prove me wrong!

Evermore,
The Condemned Warden

※※※

Intimacy is dead. Courtship is extinct. They have been replaced by desire and lust. They were victims of the technical age when relationships became more about convenience rather than commitment. Relationships stopped having depth in order to find the perfect couple's selfie to hashtag relationship goals.

Harkin laughed to himself as he watched the other customers in the coffee shop over his laptop screen. He was amused by his mental ranting because it was due to the advancement of technology that, although he was not a rich man, he was becoming comfortably wealthy. It was also why he was beginning to enjoy this particular place. He had tried a few others but was surprised in one when he realized he was being glared at for being the only one without an actual hard copy newspaper. In another, even the counter girls were on their phones enough that he could not even order.

Here, the service was friendly. There was an elderly gentleman in the corner every morning reading the paper who did not seem to care about his laptop. No one, in fact, seemed to care if he worked for three hours at a table as long as he ordered something.

"You will never find the love of your life like that!"

Harkin jumped, mildly startled by the interruption of the barista setting another coffee in front of him. He did not remember ordering any more coffee, but as he looked around the small coffee shop realized it was much emptier than he remembered, and he began to wonder how long he had been there.

"How do you know that the love of my life isn't a snarky little redhead with a talent for seeing people's caffeine fix?"

"Oh, honey! You couldn't handle me," She said with a charming smile, "besides, this is not where I go to look for my dream guy."

"And where would that be?" Harkin asked nonchalantly.

"Why? So, you can start showing up there?"

Harkin shrugged, "It sounded like a solid plan."

"Cute," She remarked, still wearing that charming smile, "So do you actually believe in all that online dating stuff?" She said, gesturing to his open laptop.

"It would be kind of wrong for me not to."

"How's that?" She asked, puzzled, "I assume you're not married if you're still trolling these sites."

"No, nothing like that. I design the algorithms that most of these sites use for their compatibility assessments. Match and eHarmony, I'm the guy that makes their computers say this guy goes to this girl."

"How about Farmer's Only?" She asked with a teasing smirk.

Harkin gave her an embarrassed grin.

"Oh, please tell me you didn't help with the jingle!" She exclaimed.

"Absolutely not!" Harkin answered quickly, then held out his hand to her, "My name's Harkin."

"Harkin?"

"Most people just call me Harry."

"I think I could do that. I'm Emilia."

"And you were giving me grief for Harkin?"

"My friends call me Emily. You can call me Em."

"Wow! I'm not sure if I should feel insulted or honored."

Emilia just winked her excessively blue eyes as she walked away. Harkin knew by the way that the other baristas were smiling at him that he must have been grinning as he watched her go. It was not a lewd or leering motivation that kept his eyes trained on her as she moved away from him. It was the way she walked. It was not proud, but it was not humbled either. Her shoulders were back, her chin was up, and her stride was confident, but he could see that it was hard-earned confidence. Something told him that the woman he was watching walk away had fought for that sunny disposition.

♣♣♣

Harkin walked into his new coffee shop office the next day and began to have another internal debate. He had started to like the place but was beginning to question how much work he would really get done, especially with her around.

Harkin had been aware of Emily since the first time he had come in. She was hard to miss even he could admit to that, but until yesterday, he had not advanced beyond exchanging the necessary pleasantries. Now seeing her smile from behind the counter when he walked in, her cornflower blue eyes that were so vibrant that they were almost too blue and sat in dark contrast to her burgundy red hair that cascaded over her shoulders.

Her melodious voice interrupted his internal debate, and he did his best to pull himself back to reality.

"So, how's romance's IT guy today?" Emily asked when Harkin walked in.

Harkin smiled, "That's good. Can I steal that for my business cards?"

"I would be offended if you didn't. Another Caramel Cloud Macchiato for you this morning?" She asked with a polite and professional voice.

"Yes, please! And can we add a chocolate croissant? I think it is going to be one of those kinds of days."

Emilia's blue eyes sparkled, "Only if you're sharing."

"If it's with you, of course, I'll share." Harkin smiled, then finished the thought in the back of his head, "If you come to have a seat with me, I will even go so far as to order one just for you."

She bit her bottom lip as if it were a serious temptation before looking back at the girls working behind her, "Give me 15 minutes."

"Deal," Harkin said, paying for all of it before pointing to the empty table he was going to sit at, and she nodded.

Emily came over with a drink carrier and two croissants fifteen minutes later, then sat down with Harkin and slid his across the table to him. He took a slow sip from his drink, watching the way Emily was using her fingers to pick at the pastry and the way her hair fell across her face as she looked down. She looked up self-consciously to see the way he was smiling quietly at her.

"I think I should tell you that this can't be a relationship," Emily said seriously.

"Of course not. That would be unprofessional." Harkin answered unphased.

"What?" Emily asked, confused.

"I can't be dating my secretary."

"Secretary?"

"I come here to work. It's kind of like my office. You bring me my coffee and croissants. So, it does kind of make you my secretary. Don't worry, though. I won't make you screen my calls." Harkin finished with a smile.

"Ha-ha. I'm being serious." She replied scathingly.

"I know. Forgive a guy for trying to lighten the blow?" He asked with a half shrug.

"I suppose." She replied with a sweet smile.

"Can I ask why? And please, don't do the 'it's not you, it's me' thing."

"Well, it's true!" Emily protested.

Harkin did not say anything but only raised an eyebrow at her as he took another drink.

"I can't be in a relationship right now. It really has nothing to do with you. It's not healthy for me."

"Ah, at least you didn't try to tell me I seem like a nice guy and all."

"Would that really be so bad?" She asked seriously.

Harkin frowned.

"Alright. Alright." She relented.

"Can I ask... why would it be unhealthy?"

"Promise not to get weird about it?" She asked, looking him over appraisingly.

"No more than I already have. Promise."

Emily smiled, "My sponsor says I'm in a place of my recovery that relationships could be dangerous and cause a relapse."

Harkin nodded, "So, what does your sponsor say about friends?"

"Really? That's it?" She asked in disbelief.

Harkin shrugged, "I have questions, don't mistake that, but if we have time, I figured I would ask them when you were more comfortable."

Picking at her chocolate croissant, she met his eyes with another smile, "You mean you're going to ply me with chocolate, don't you?"

"What else are friends for?"

"Seriously though, no normal guy is this chill about finding out that a pretty girl used to be a junkie. What's your deal?"

"Hmm." Harkin paused, giving her a speculative look, "I don't recall saying pretty."

"Nice! It was inferred." She said contemptuously as he laughed at the look on her face.

She leaned back in her chair, crossed her legs, then sipped her drink. She peered at him over the rim of the cup, and her blue eyes drew his eyes to hers.

"So, for real, what's your deal?" She asked again.

Harkin shrugged, thinking about his answer. Was it as simple as he was just glad to hear a deeper truth? How could he explain that he was tired of the 150 words or less bios that usually started with something about long walks that he had to thumb through to gather data when he was reconfiguring the algorithms?

He leaned back in the chair to look around the little café.

"No one is getting you out of this." She teased, "Come on, fess up."

Harkin sighed, "Got time for a story?"

"Sure."

"A few months ago, one of the companies that I consult for called me about a lawsuit that a couple was attempting to bring against them."

"Did you have something to do with it?" She interrupted.

Harkin jerked his head in a noncommittal gesture, "Only so much as they mostly thought I would find it amusing and as I was technically working for the company at the time, so they were not breaking any laws by sharing the details. Anyway, back to the story. This married couple was stepping out on one another, and neither knew the other was being unfaithful until they each used the services of my employer."

"You make it sound like you work for the mob." Emilia snorted.

"Oh no," Harkin dry-panned, "these people are much worse. Always messy, and I have to sign all kinds of non-disclosures. These people made racketeering legal."

She laughed.

"Anyway," He said, pointedly, "this couple found out that their spouse was cheating on them when their compatibility profiles revealed they were a near-perfect match for one another, and they had met for a date."

"No." Emilia drawled in stunned disbelief.

"Yes, but, wait, it gets better. Rather than seeking a dissolution of marriage, they became a united front and tried to sue the company for false advertising as there was no way their compatibility assessments were correct."

"You're joking?"

Harkin shook his head.

"Okay, so what does this have to do with me, and how you're totally cool about all that?"

"That couple. All the rest like them. They are just numbers in a collected set of data for me. After you get used to seeing people as data, they stop being real, and when people aren't real, they don't surprise you."

"That's a bit... serial killer-ish," Emily remarked.

"Promise not to get weird?" Harkin asked with a smirk.

She shook her head, "I get it, though. It is similar when you first get clean. It feels like drowning. Life just has a way of pulling you under. It's not like... the whole colors are brighter, and the air is fresher crap like the movies make it seem, you know, there is just this teetering feeling between melancholy and apathy that you just settle over."

Emilia stopped talking and was giving Harkin an amused smirk. He realized he was staring at her, with his cup frozen halfway to his mouth in the middle of the process of taking a drink. Her words had resonated far deeper than he would have expected. In truth, she had just surprised him. She had become real.

"You know what I'm talking about, don't you?" Emilia asked, her demeanor slipping between amusement and suspicion.

"Everyone has their vices," Harkin said in the way of an answer, "whether they're alcoholics or addicts."

"No, you're not a drinker. There isn't enough self-loathing in you for that. Just the hatred of it."

Again, Harkin was staring at her, unaware that he was frozen in surprise.

As if reading his thoughts, she leaned forward and whispered conspiratorially, "Am I still just a number on a spreadsheet? A data point in one of your compatibility assessments?"

"No." He answered in the same whisper.

Her vibrant blue eyes winked at him as she leaned away from the table and uncrossed her legs.

"Thank you for lunch," She said as she stood to her feet collecting her trash from the table, "I'll come by and give you a warm-up later, but you need to work."

Before she could turn to walk away, Harkin asked, "Just to be clear before you get my hopes up, are you talking about giving me a warm-up or my cup?"

"Well, let's just see how productive you are, and we'll go from there." Emilia said with another wink.

Harkin felt like he had hit a stride in his work when she sat down at the table again.

"Is it time for that warm-up?" He asked.

Emilia gave him a bewildered smile, "You've had four. I actually came to see if you wanted to walk me home?"

At first, Harkin did not answer. He was busy staring at his cup as if trying to remember when it had been refilled. Then the rest of what she said seemed to break through his thoughts.

"Doesn't that go against that strict policy of yours?" He asked.

"Don't get ahead of yourself. It's not like I will be inviting you in or anything. Friends walk together, don't they?"

"I don't know. I can't say I've had a lot of friends and certainly not the walking kind." Harkin replied.

"Well me neither. So, we'll be those kinds of friends. Now, are you going to put that stuff away and walk with me or not?"

"Yes, ma'am."

"Don't ever do that again." She warned with mock severity.

This time, he winked, "Of course not."

The walk together was friendly, Harkin decided. She had run her arm through his, but it still felt somehow casual enough that he did not feel it was anything more than an almost unconscious gesture, and he smiled to himself when she stopped in front of a door no more than a block away from the coffee shop. Then without a word, Emily stood on her toes then kissed him suddenly. Her fingers digging into the fabric of his shirt. Harkin was just beginning to break his surprise and lean into the kiss when she broke it.

She starred at her fingers which were now absentmindedly smoothing his shirt. Emily was chewing on her bottom lip, then she let it slip through her teeth, the motion leaving white tracks from her teeth on her skin. The action made Harkin want to kiss her again.

"That doesn't help the whole 'let's be friends' thing, does it?"

"I'm afraid not." He replied.

"Don't suppose you could just forget about it?"

Harkin gave her a bemused frown, "Not seeming likely."

Despite herself, Emily smiled then said, "I'm sorry, but really I can't. Not right now."

Harkin reached up then removed her hand from his shirt before taking a step back, "I'm not the one challenging that."

He did not sound mad, Emily thought, or agitated. In fact, Harkin did not even seem disappointed to her. Emily thought he sounded only compassionate then wondered if it was something else.

"I'm really sorry." She repeated.

Harkin sighed dejectedly, "So am I. I was really starting to like that coffee shop."

"What?" She asked suspiciously.

"Well, I obviously can't keep going back there to work if you find me so irresistible. Not if it's going to cause you problems."

Emily was staring at him, unaware that she had let her mouth open slightly in disbelief. Harkin winked at her, finally breaking his straight face with a smile.

"Seriously," Harkin started in a gentle tone, "despite the common belief, I am an adult. If you don't want to do this, I can respect that. I'm happy to let you serve me coffee with a smile, and if my eyes linger on you a little longer while you walk away," Harkin shrugged, "that's the beginning and end of it. So be it."

"Just like that?" Emilia asked.

"Just like that." Harkin affirmed.

"Did I just stop being real to you?" She asked.

"No, it's worse than that," Emily answered for him in his silence, "I became just another addict."

"No," Harkin said, a stern, crisp edge to his voice, "you became a friend. That is all."

He nodded his head and walked away, being careful not to brush against her. Emilia watched after him as he left, completely unaware of how painfully deep those final three words had cut her. She began to unlock her door and missed Harkin stop at the street corner to look back at her.

***

To My Unkindled Love,

It was never about admitting powerlessness. Yes, that was where it ended but it was about recognizing something so much more. It was about recognizing sin. A word you have done your best to avoid, I know. You still want to use words like temptation or addiction, occasionally you will admit it as a mistake even, but it all goes back to sin. So, before we go any further, this is where you take the hit and call it what it is. This is where you face up to the monster under all the masks.

Dear child, this is not to be harsh or cruel. This is about giving you the best chance and all the best hope, but in order to do that, in order for the light at the end of the tunnel to look the brightest is because you have to see the darkness of the tunnel first. This is about admitting that you have let sin do nearly irreparable damage. Actually, it has done so much damage you cannot fix it alone. This is where you admit powerlessness so that you can be humbled. Because, sweet darling, only when you have been humbled are you willing to accept help. That is why it is important to recognize sin so that you can seek proper help, and I do mean proper help. There are a great many other things in which help is implied without being meant, and as painful as it is to recall, I know you are aware of exactly what I refer to. So, proper help is very important.

Proper help is needed in order to face proper sin. After all, you know, the proper face of sin is only a reflection. The surface of a mirror shimmers and shines, but it still only reflects what it is shown. You know what it will always show, and you know someone felt the same. You've read that verse, "For I know that nothing good dwells in me, that is, in my flesh; for the willing is

present in me, but the doing of the good is not."
Romans 7:18

Your sin comes from you; a duality of wanting to do good and to do what feels good even when the two are at ends of one another. My sweet darling child, you have spent quite a bit of time just trying to do what feels good, and I say that passing no judgment or reproach, but now it is time to do what IS good. This is where you admit that powerlessness to not be able to make that distinction alone. You confess because you cannot overcome you by yourself.

Evermore,
Your Kindred Heart

Chapter Two

To whom it may concern;

I suppose that is the best way to address this since I never know who it's for. Am I doing this for some future self-edification? Or even what version of myself do I even hope will read this? Do I ever want this to be read? I wish I knew, but I doubt that knowledge would make this any easier. Knowledge before edification rarely leads to revelation, and edification before knowledge rarely leads to gratification. Those are interesting concepts for you to be searching out: revelation and gratification. You haven't even put self in front of them: self-revelation and self-gratification. I know at least one of those you are familiar with.

Is that your intent? To forget yourself? To find some revelation or gratification without loathing, self or otherwise? It would be easier if I even knew the intent. Ambition, love, despair; all good candidates, and yet I think they all fall far short of the prize. Of course, to no fault of their own. They all are good sentiments and worthy of a letter, I have no doubt. Just not this letter. No, you have far greater reasons for this letter. I almost dare to call it purpose, but you are not accustomed to what that would really imply. Purpose is something you, my friend, lack in no small measure because purpose is intensely intent, and you are not. The truth of the matter is I do not know your intent.

Funny, though, that I, of all people, should be the one to speak of the truth of matters. Me. The one who cannot even answer questions like "how are you" without even one littlest of white lies. Honesty and truth were never my forte, exactly. Honestly, I don't remember a time when they ever came easy. So, if truth is of some import to you, bear with me. After all, maybe we can find some kind of selfless revelation or gratification if we only had an intent or purpose or truth.

Evermore,
The Humblest of Liars

***

The woman's dark complexion made an exquisite backdrop to her emerald green eyes to the point that Emilia would have described her one-time friend as exotic. Her long curly, light ash brown hair that used to fall past her shoulders was now shortened to what could now only be called a prison cut. Yet, Emily thought, she still looked radiant to her. She still looked healthier than the last time Emily could remember seeing her. Even under the harsh lights, her friend was beautiful.

"Hey, Emi!" The woman said cheerfully with a slightly hindered wave.

"Hi," Emily said hesitantly sitting down, "how are you, Misty?"

Emily could see Misty's cheerful demeanor slip slightly.

"You didn't want to come, did you?" Misty asked, and Emily wondered if there was some bitterness in it.

"I wasn't sure you wanted me to." Emily answered truthfully.

"But it's you who has been putting money in my commissary fund. I'm sure of it."

"Yes, it's been me." Emily admitted.

"Then, why did you think I didn't want to see you?" Misty asked.

Emily chewed her lower lip before answering, "Because you're in here, and I'm not. I thought you might blame me."

Misty was shaking her head with a certain level of pity, "This isn't your fault. Don't be so egotistical. I'm here because of me, and I'm clean because of this place, so I can't resent anyone for that."

"If you hadn't tried to drive me to the hospital, you wouldn't..." Emily trailed off as Misty held up her hand.

"I didn't try. I got you to the hospital, and if I hadn't, you would be dead. Maybe both of us would have been, and I don't know on the cosmic scale of things, if two junkies would have been worth that boy's life, but look at you now. They get you to rehab? You clean?"

"Yes, and yes. Since I was left on the sidewalk in front of the hospital, I was put on suicide watch when I was first admitted, but yeah, they got me in a clinic."

Misty shrugged, "I got you to the hospital. As high as we were, I think we should just be glad I didn't drop you off in front of a burger king."

Emily smiled, "Thank you."

"Is that why you've been giving me money? You felt guilty?" Misty asked. This time Emily was sure she heard a hint of anger in her voice.

"Not just guilty. If it wasn't for you, I know I would be dead. I'm grateful. There isn't much I could do, but I wanted to do something."

"Well, I'm glad you didn't try to bake me anything." Misty joked.

"Ha-ha." Emily playfully chided before pressing on, "Really, how are you?"

"I'm good, Emi. Really. This is more of a white-collar prison. Mostly nonviolent drug-related crimes. People like me who didn't mean to hurt anyone but were too high or too drunk to keep from killing someone. And, there are some girls who are in here for like embezzlement stuff. It's not as bad as you think. Think more of a rehab you can't leave."

"Misty?"

"Emi."

"What happened? Do you remember?" Emily asked hesitantly.

"I wasn't as high as you were, but it's kind of fuzzy."

"What do you remember?"

"You shot up that last time. I freaked when I couldn't wake you up. Then you started shaking. I drove you to the hospital, but then I got scared that they would know I was high, and I know how it sounds now, but then it made sense. So, I didn't take you inside. Then after I left you at the hospital, I ran through an intersection." At this, Misty's voice broke, and she swallowed but kept talking, "I hit him in the driver's side. They told me after the fact that he was dead when the paramedics arrived and I was unconscious. He was twenty-two coming home from school for the weekend." Misty wiped at her eyes, "He was studying to be a high school history teacher."

"How do you know that?" Emily asked.

"Part of making amends. I reached out to his family. They actually responded. His mother actually came up here. They pulled us to a separate room normally used for lawyers. They do really encourage recovery here. Anyway, she talked to me for a while, and she showed me pictures. He was a handsome kid." Misty smiled in a painfully wistful way.

"Uh. Did she forgive you?" Emily asked cautiously.

"No," Misty answered flatly, "but she did say that she was pleased to see that I was clean. She also said that she hoped her son's death would serve as a good reminder for me to stay that way."

"Wow!"

"Yeah, it was heavy. But she was on to something with that. I think we need something heavy to help us stay clean."

"Time's up." A guard called behind Misty.

"Oh," Misty said with a half glance over her shoulder, "Are you coming back?"

"If it's okay with you?"

"I think I would like that, but if you don't want to, you can do that instead." Misty said with a smile as she gestured to a piece of paper on the table, "The guard put it there for you. I'm not allowed to touch it. They have this video phone thing they can do." Misty leaned forward to whisper, "It is okay if you don't want to come in here."

Emily picked up the paper with the information on it, "I just set it up from my phone at home, and then what?" she asked, reading through it.

"They will take me to one of the video monitors in the other room at the appointed time you select. Then I will hit the call button or whatever, and you will get a video call from me."

"Then I will see you soon. Bye."

"Bye."

***

Emily sat in the old, weathered chair in front of the desk, playing with her fingers distractedly. The older gentleman sitting across the desk from her leaned back in his office chair patiently, a small comforting, understanding smile pulling at the corners of his lips. When she finally looked up to meet his eyes, she saw there was still a simple kind of love twinkling behind them.

Emily only had a vague recollection of the first time she had met this man. She had been in the hospital coming back from the worst side effects of withdrawal. She had still been restrained to the hospital bed since she was still under a seventy-two hour suicide watch. The restraints were loose enough that she could turn so that she did not choke on her own vomit but not loose enough to allow her to leave or reach one wrist with the other hand. She could see a young lady sitting outside the door serving as a patient observer, watching her casually over the top of her book. That was when this man walked in. He had been crisply but not too formally dressed. He had introduced himself when he came into the room carrying a bible. All Emily had remembered was that he had introduced himself as a hospital chaplain and she had panicked thinking that he had come to perform last rites. After all, she felt like she was dying.

When he had calmed her down, he informed her she was going to live, but he asked her what kind of quality of life she expected to have. He had told her that she had nearly overdosed on an illegal substance, and without someone coming to take responsibility for her, it was possible that she would be remanded to the county whether, in a general lockup or a drug rehabilitation clinic, he was not sure. Then, he gave her an option. He told her about a fully funded drug recovery problem that he could make available to her if she was willing to give it an honest shot. When she asked why he would do that, he told her his faith believed strongly that everyone deserves a chance for redemption.

Now, here she sat in front of him in their agreed weekly meetings for the first year after she was allowed to leave the clinic and live on her own to make sure she was reacclimating safely to a new drug-free lifestyle.

"I went to see her." Emily finally said.

"Good, and?" He pressed softly.

"She looks really good. Like healthy. I think she is even more beautiful." Emily rambled.

"I don't doubt it. I've told you that you shine a little brighter every day. The drugs and the chemicals have a way of diminishing that glow the longer you take them, but it comes back if you get them out of your system. So, what did you two talk about?"

"I asked her what happened." Emily said cautiously.

"That's good," He reassured, "it is only natural that you would want closure. Did she tell you?"

"Yes."

"And?"

"She left me on the sidewalk because she was afraid of the hospital realizing she was high," Emily stopped, but he only nodded and gestured for her to continue, "she made the joke that it was a good thing she made it to the hospital and not a burger king." Emily said with a small laugh, "I don't know how true that is. I don't think she was that high, but really who am I to judge. I don't even remember that night."

The gentleman leaned forward, crossing his arms on his desk to look closely at her, "And did she tell you why she was in there?"

Emily looked down at her fingers again and sighed before answering, "She was in a car accident leaving the hospital. She said that she hit another driver and he was dead when the paramedics arrived."

"And how does that make you feel?" He asked gently.

"Like it's my fault he's dead, and she's in there." Emily answered.

"But do you believe that?"

"No. She told me it wasn't my fault, and I believe her," Emily hesitated, and he seemed to know so she finished what she was thinking, "she said this thing about balancing on a cosmic scale. It made me think about how you always talk about God's plan in everything."

He nodded with an approving smile, "I think that is a very good comparison. I don't know how her rehabilitation is focused, but it does sound like what we have been discussing. Are you going to go see her again?"

Emily pulled the folded piece of paper out of her handclasp, "She told me I could do this if I didn't want to go in there again. Do you think it would be a good idea?"

He put on a pair of reading glasses to look over the paper she handed him, then sat in on the desk before taking his glasses off and sitting them on it, "Normally, in a recovery program, it is discouraged to keep friends from that lifestyle. There is peer pressure and routine that makes it easier to fall into those old ways. However, she is currently incarcerated and undergoing a recovery program herself, so she has been removed from the lifestyle herself. I would actually think that you pose a greater danger to her recovery than she does to yours, emotionally anyway. But and this is the important thing, you two are actually taking this journey together right now. It is very possible that this could be very good for both of you; not just to have a friendship or something like a sponsor who has been there and knows the pitfalls and challenges but also accountability." He picked up the piece of paper and handed it back to her, "If this is something you want to do, I would cautiously encourage it."

"Thank you."

"Emilia, don't thank me. I still strongly recommend caution. This does have the potential to be harmful to either one of you girls. Don't forget that, but it could be beneficial. Understand, I will be asking about this relationship more as you choose to let it progress." Emily nodded, and he sighed contently, "Now, anything else happen this week that we should take about?"

When Emily did not immediately answer but bit her lip, he frowned before speaking in a slightly sterner voice, "Complete, open honesty. Remember, Emilia."

"I know." She consented, "I know you said a relationship right now could be dangerous, but what about friendships?"

There was a mixture of a confused worry play across his features as he measured out his next response, "Friendships are cautiously encouraged. Understand, you have to learn how to healthily deal with emotional responses, so you do need friends, but you have to be careful not to become too overly attached to them that a fight or argument or whatever else drives you back to old habits. However, I think you're implying that this friendship is a little different already."

"It's this guy I met at work. He's one of the customers."

He looked disapprovingly as he asked, "What happened?"

"I told him we could just be friends, and he said that was okay. He bought me lunch on my lunch break. We talked, and it was just fun and relaxing."

"What did you tell him for a reason why you could only be friends?" He asked with a curious expression playing across his face.

"That I was a recovering addict." Emily answered honestly.

"And, that's when he said what?"

"That's when he asked about just being friends."

He nodded before speaking again, "So you are wondering if it's okay to keep being friends with this guy since that little fact about your past didn't scare him off?"

"Yes, mostly."

"What do you mean "mostly"?" He asked suspiciously.

"I let him walk me home, and I kissed him, but then I apologized and told him that I couldn't be more than friends again, and he said he wasn't the one challenging that." Emily sighed, "What do I do?"

He chuckled, "Sounds like an interesting fellow. Do you really think that he is alright with just being friends?"

Emily was silent for a moment thinking, "Yes. I don't know what it is, but there is this thing about him like he understands what it feels like to be sober again, but he doesn't seem to have a drug history. It is more of a callousness towards life. I think he is truly okay with just being friends."

"If that is true, then I would be willing to suggest let you continue to feel this friendship out, but if it gets to be overwhelming, then you need to step back. I still don't think you are in a good place to be considering a relationship yet. Your recovery is making tremendous progress, but I think it is still in a fragile place, at least enough of one that I don't want you testing it yet. Are you okay with that?" Emily nodded, "Okay, is there anything else you need to discuss this week?"

"I don't think so." Emily answered tentatively.

"Then I will let you go. So, you are going to pursue a friendship with," He paused thinking, then picked up again, "Misty through the proper channels of communication, and you may continue to talk with this gentleman at work." He paused, making a couple of notes in her appointment block for next week, "I will be asking about these next week to see how you are handling them. Have a wonderful day, Emilia. And remember to call if you need anything. You don't have to wait until next week."

"Thank you."

***

To My Unkindled Love,

Coming to the understanding that you cannot overcome you by yourself opens the door to admitting you need something more than yourself, and that brings us back to the heart of believing there is a power greater than ourselves. You have to decide who God is to you! You have to decide the relationship you will have with Him! God can restore your sanity. He can give you hope when you have none. He can piece your life back together and renew you. He is the stronger power outside of you that can help you overcome yourself. That in itself is the power! My dear child, I know pop culture cautions great power and great responsibility, but that is only because pop culture breeds fear. Great power is not a responsibility; it is a fulcrum. A tool. Power is God giving you the leverage to overcome you.

You've heard it clearly defined already, "For God is working in you, giving you the desire and the power to do what pleases HIM." Philippians 2:13 (NASB)

You are given the power to break away from sin. You are given the power to do good, to do what pleases Him. God is working in you to give you that power and ability but also that desire. He is giving you the leverage to move the weight that is holding you down and holding you back. His power is the fulcrum upon which the duality of your soul rest, and the longer you stay balanced at the pivotal point, the longer you remain powerless.

God is removing from you that powerlessness and also giving you the desire to improve you and beyond you, but only if you make a decision. You have to decide who God is to you and the relationship you will have with Him.

Evermore,

Your Kindred Heart

Chapter Three

To whom it may concern;

So promising! As if it may concern anyone but you. I'm not even sure it concerns you anymore. Then again, maybe it concerns you even more. Perhaps it concerns you because you are waiting to see how far you will unravel letter by letter, word by word, all the way down to every last punctuation. I guess maybe you could stave off that worry. I suppose you could start addressing them to God and make these letters one more tool to strengthen that relationship like they talk about, but you've already tried that before, haven't you? It made it all just a little too formal. It is hard to yell and be honest when you are worried about remaining reverent. Some things you just can't say respectfully.

There it is again, that word, not respect. I know how much you've heard that lately. Respect the space, respect their perspective, self-respect, respect the process—screw respect. No, I'm talking about the other word. Honest. I'm no Sherlock, but I'm starting to notice a theme here, and denial doesn't suit you, my friend. Terrifying, isn't it? When all the voices in your head agree but don't worry, that is only a surface problem. If you were to really listen to them, you would see that they cannot even agree as to why you should be honest. They all keep screaming for you to be honest with yourself, but they can't seem to remember why you need to be honest or why you were lying to start with. I'm not even sure you know what you're hiding anymore, but go ahead, be honest.

In all of this, my only concern is asking, do you even know who you should be honest to? Yourself? In what capacity? Someone else? Who and why? And, of course, the kicker, for what intent? Remember friend, truth is nothing if not intentional. And you? Have you ever been intentional? Lying is not an intentional thing. Just so you know, lying is a tactic to avoid intentions and commitments.

Evermore,

The Voice of Deranged Reason

***

"Wow! Look at you." Emily said, looking up to see Harkin entering the shop.

Harkin froze at the counter then looked down at himself, "What?"

"Never seen you in a tie before. Finally, find the right profile with all the trolling?" She asked with a smirk.

He frowned with concern, "Too much?"

"Oh, please tell me you're joking!" Emily exclaimed.

"Yeah. It's just a couple of important errands."

She sat his drink on the counter, "That wasn't funny."

Harkin shrugged, "You started it."

"What are you? Four?"

"Four and three quarters." Harkin said in a mockingly prideful tone.

Emily laughed hard enough that she had hidden her mouth behind her hand. The way her blue eyes sparkled when she laughed made Harkin smile broader. Emily noticed his smile as she laughed, but she did not comment on it. When she got control of herself, she saw the way his seriousness bled through his smile.

"You alright?" She asked.

"Just going to be a long day, but you've made it better." Harkin answered solemnly.

"It's just caffeine."

"Oh, yeah, that too." He said with a smirk picking up his cup, "Keep smiling for me today." Harkin called out as he walked back to the door.

Two hours later, Harkin grabbed the flowers off of his passenger seat and started a slow walk across the nicely kept lawn.

***

He never used the word brooding. All of his friends did, but Benjamin never did. That was the way of it with Benjamin though, he had a mind for thought but never had a mouth for words. Do not misunderstand. He was not mute, nor was he sparing with his words, but there was a way about him that said he was comfortably at peace in the quiet times.

That, more than anything, was what set him apart and what unsettled those who learned the workings of his mind. There is a phrase for that distinction. Speak now or forever hold your peace. It was funny to Benjamin how that is the one line, the one time, that a room full of people can be given an ultimatum and not be offended. It is the one time that a pastor can issue a challenge without angering anyone. Benjamin had a way of understanding the magnitude of the moment, the importance of the intention, the choice to raise his voice and risk everything or stay silent and live with regret. No one man stands at the cusp of that pivotal moment without first thinking about it, but men like Benjamin chose to live there, so when he spoke, his words were always measured to face that abyss.

As time passed, Benjamin would have called himself a grave-digger and he would have been proud of the profession. Now, he just told people he was a groundskeeper. It was easier. Nobody thought that a fifty-seven-year-old man should have so easily turned to such a career. They all held the opinion eighteen years ago that it was too soon for him to have chosen such a career and claim that he had no need to dream further. After all, nobody respected the shadow that dug the hole with machinery that was hidden during the ceremony at the graveside. Nobody respected the man that was there to make sure the marker was placed properly. Well, that was not necessarily true. Nobody gave him much thought, actually.

That was possibly why sometimes, when time was not so pressed, he did not use the machinery. Benjamin, wearing his old denim overalls and work shirt, would carry his shovel flung over his shoulder out behind the little church, and he would dig the grave. He would lay out a tarp next to the hole to catch the dirt and not damage the grass, and he would spend an afternoon, sometimes two, digging a grave for a stranger. He would pour his sweat into their final resting place because he knew that sometimes that was the most respect they were going to get.

"Hi-ho, hi-ho!" Sang a trilling voice behind him.

Klarissa was a church songbird, in Benjamin's mind. She never sang from the choir perch, but whenever she sang, her voice filled the church. She was a twenty-five-year-old woman with a past that Benjamin did not like to think about, nor did he feel comfortable speaking of. She always smiled; he noticed that. It was framed by her sunny blonde hair that sat in sharp contrast to her emerald eyes. In the last five years of coming to the church, she had become a strong leader with the youth and a wonderful teacher to the children.

Klarissa settled on a corner of the tarp not covered in dirt, seemingly not worried about tarnishing her jeans or t-shirt.

"Good afternoon, sir." Klarissa said.

"Miss." Benji replied, still standing in a shoulder-deep squared-off hole; he knew it was six feet when it came level with his eyes.

"Doesn't the church have a backhoe for this?" she asked.

"Yes."

Klarissa sighed patiently, "Then why don't you use it? I mean, I saw you out here yesterday digging too. Wouldn't it have been easier?"

"The last act ever done for you on this earth. Would you want it to be easy?" Benjamin asked.

"I expect that's probably the way it will be done, but I guess it's not what I would want. So, you knew them?"

"No."

This time, Klarissa's sigh was a little less patient, "Is there a reason you don't like to explain yourself to me specifically?"

"I have no dislike of that at all, miss. I just don't wish to add to your burden."

"Care to explain, or am I supposed to guess what you mean by that?" she asked.

Benjamin leaned his shovel against the grave wall then rested his elbows on the edge as he peered at her. This time, it was his turn to sigh.

"You tell the story of David and Goliath to the children, yes?" Benjamin asked.

"I do."

"Tell it to me, the way you would to them."

"I don't see how this helps." She remarked.

"You'll have my answer, but it will be a time in coming. Please."

"Um, I talk about the boy who faces an army's champion and wins. I talk about the speech he gives on how God saw him through other threats in his life. How does this help?"

"Do you ever talk about the pressure?"

"Pressure?" Klarissa repeated.

"He was a young man when he went to face Goliath. He stepped up as the champion of an army, and he may have had God's backing, but he did not even have his brother's. How many of the men there truly believed and supported him? Oh, faith can say a great many things, but even if David knew he was going to succeed through God, he still felt pressure."

"Interesting. Do you not believe that even the king supported him?"

"The king was desperate."

"Then you think I have no support?" Klarissa asked testily.

"I know that you do, but I don't want support to feel like a burden. To anyone."

"Just a grave-digger?" Klarissa remarked.

Benjamin did not answer but reached for his shovel again. It was not a dismissive gesture, not anything impolite. In fact, it was a fluid, relaxed movement that seemed to put them both at ease. Klarissa had seen the stiffly well-mannered act enough from Benjamin that to see him comfortable seemed a rare thing.

"Can I ask you something?" Klarissa asked.

"If you feel you must."

"Do you ever worry about one caving in on you when you dig them this way?"

Benjamin emptied his shovel on the tarp, mindful not to throw dirt onto her, then he let their eyes meet.

"Not anymore."

"It happened?" She asked in shock.

"Once."

"Oh, come on! Tell me about it." She exclaimed.

At first, Benjamin did not say anything but stooped down. Klarissa thought that he was digging, but he did not straighten back up, nor did she hear the scrape of his shovel.

"Sir?" She called, leaning forward over the grave.

Sitting at the bottom with his back against the wall and his legs stretched in front of him, Benjamin held his arms out with a shrug.

"I used to sit like this for lunch, and one day the wall shifted. It buried me. Physically, all you feel is pressure. There is a moment of fear that you will suffocate, but luckily around my head, the dirt was thin, and I could breathe. Shallowly. It was still hard to push my chest out enough to draw breath, but I managed."

"How long were you like that?"

"Almost two days. My arms were too buried to dig myself out. A man passing through to visit a loved one happens to notice me and dug me out."

"And you still do this?" She asked, moving away from the edge of the grave, afraid of the idea of causing it to cave in, "Get up! Don't sit like that!" She exclaimed.

For the first time, she saw Benjamin smile as he stood to his feet, "Hey, you asked."

"That's right, I did. Why do you still do this?" She repeated.

"Dig the graves? Or, do it by hand?" Benjamin asked.

"Umm, both."

"I'm okay if I dig my own grave, and at least this way, I know it was done properly."

"That's all?"

"I ain't preaching, miss."

"Okay. That's enough of that."

Without another moment of hesitation for either of them, Klarissa jumped into the grave with him. The edge of the grave was level with her brow so that she had to look up in order to see out of the grave, and Benjamin could see that chill crawl across her skin.

"Now what?" He asked softly.

"Why do you do this? Can you not feel this?" She said, rubbing her palms on her arms as if she were in heavy winter snow without a coat.

Benjamin placed a hand on her arm with a sympathetic expression, "You shouldn't have done that. Can you climb out, or do you need help?"

It was another terrifying moment for Klarissa. She felt his hand and felt nothing at the same time. As a shadow meets darkness, she felt no warmth from his skin as it touched her already chilled skin.

"No, you first. Why?"

"I am more comfortable here than anywhere else. I have no one here waiting on me to speak to them."

"Does anyone?"

"Yes. These graves are filled with people who died waiting to hear someone tell them what they waited all their lives to hear, and so many times, I have come here to see loved ones trying to say those words too late. It may be weddings we hear it most, but this is where we see it played out."

"What?"

"Speak now or forever hold your peace. This is where we see action and regret lived out, and this is where we see them all die. I don't feel disquieted by this. I feel at peace. That is why I do it." He gestured to the edge, "Now, do you need help out?"

"How are you going to do it? Please don't leave me in here by myself."

"Of course not." Benjamin knelt down, "Step onto my knee, then onto my shoulder, and you should be able to get out from there."

"Won't that hurt?" He raised an eyebrow at her, and it was the closest she had seen to him smirk, "Oh, alright!"

She gently stepped onto his knee, then his shoulder mumbling an apology even though he seemed unconcerned by it. Once she had hoisted herself over the edge, she backed away toward the corner of the tarp again. She sat quietly, pulling at a piece of grass in her hands.

"Miss?"

"I don't like it." Klarissa muttered.

"It's the job."

"No, I meant, I really don't like that you keep calling me 'miss.'" She corrected.

Benjamin finally gave her a full smile, "You're going to have to tolerate it. You're getting too old for me to still call you little miss. Anyway, let me try it again. Imagine when you sit at the cusp of achievement because then it is easy to say whatever it takes. That the end will justify the means, but what about when you stand on the edges of failure. It is whatever it takes or just whatever you have left?"

Klarissa gave him an astonished look, but Benjamin kept speaking before she could interrupt, "What happens when you are not David in the scenario? When you're the army that has been cowering from the challenge? When you're the brother asking why he's even here? When you cannot even be the king trying to give him something to fight with going forward that he doesn't even really need, but you were just trying to do something?" Benjamin nodded his head toward the gentleman walking through the cemetery at a distance from them with flowers in his hand, "Then you end up like that man. You have a lot to say, but you can only say it to the people who don't need to hear it now."

"That sounds like a pretty good sermon for not preaching," Klarissa remarked absentmindedly.

***

"Hi, sis. Happy Birthday." Harkin said, placing the flowers into the carved-out vase of the headstone.

Nora Lindsey died at the age of thirteen due to complications that arose from a car accident. She had spent weeks fading in and out of consciousness due to a brain bleed that finally ended with her slipping into a coma and onto life support. Harkin still remembered sitting beside her hospice bed those last two months. He had nearly had to do his sophomore year of school over because he had stopped going choosing instead to stay by her side. By then, she slept mostly, but he told himself that she could feel his presence that it would comfort her to see him when she opened her eyes. His parents had not cared that he was not going to school. It had almost seemed like they did not care at all. In some way, he had realized that they had given up hope, that they had accepted fate. His mother spent most of the time locked in her bedroom while Nora was lying in bed in the front room, and occasionally his father would walk over to the bed, placing his hand on Harkin's shoulder as he looked down on his daughter, then he would silently walk away after a few minutes. Harkin had wondered then what his father was often thinking in those few moments.

By the time the funeral came, he did not care anymore what his father had been thinking. Both of his parents had stopped crying by then, and they seemed to go through the motions out of some respectful formality for the process, and he knew since the day of the funeral that they had not visited Nora once. Harkin made sure to bring her flowers every year on her birthday and sometimes more. Sometimes, he would sit silently and stare at the way her name was carved into the stone, and others he would talk to her like she was still that vital little girl.

Today, he sat silently a part of him admiring the shine that reflected off the stone.

"I've been doing my best to keep her looking pretty." Benjamin said behind him.

"Hey, Benji. I thought maybe you would be too busy to stop by today." Harkin said, looking over his shoulder at the groundskeeper then letting his eyes flick to the woman still standing next to the freshly dug grave.

"You were hoping, you mean." Benjamin said with a laugh.

Harkin chuckled, "I suppose. Did you clean the headstone?" Harkin asked, pointing at it.

Benjamin shrugged, "I cleaned it last night before I left. I thought she might like to look nice for her big brother when he came to see her on her birthday."

"Thank you." Harkin said, his voice breaking into a husky growl of gratitude, "Certainly doesn't look like she is fit for the ground crew." Harkin added, nodding toward the woman as a way of a distraction.

"I suppose not. I think she is just curious about the methods. Either that or for a grave-digger, I am making too many friends out here."

Harkin smiled, "You would think they would be sparing in your line of work."

"Says the guy whose only friend is the grave-digger." Benjamin replied as he sat down next to Harkin, "And no, they still haven't come by, if that was going to be your next question."

"It wasn't I've given up on them, Benji."

"Now, don't say that, Mr. Lindsey." It was the mocked formality that caused Harkin to look at him with a confused look, "Now that I have gotten your attention, I should remind you not everyone can walk these grounds like they already belong here, and not everybody can express love to those who have gone on like you can."

"They could have done it before she died. They spent her last months avoiding her. They gave up first."

Benjamin shook his head at the familiar conversation but did not reply this time. He knew it would not do any good for a wound this old. Then he decided to say something that for the years he had known Harkin he had not dared to say before.

"Do you think your sister would want you bringing your hatred to her? I imagine until the day she died, she felt loved by your parents, and she loved them. What do you think it would do for her to hear you talk this way? You think that she would feel it was her fault?"

Benjamin watched as Harkin's jaw clenched, and there was steel in his eyes, but he did not say anything until the moment passed. When Harkin spoke, there was still an edge to his voice.

"It's not her fault, but she should know what they are really like."

Benjamin stood then rested his hand on Harkin's shoulder before saying, "Maybe she is the one who really does know."

Without waiting for a response, Benjamin returned to the grave where Klarissa still sat watching him.

✳✳✳

To My Unkindled Love,

Making a decision to have a relationship with God means making a decision to turn your life and your will over to God as you understand Him. That means taking action to surrender to that power with your heart, mind, and will. It is no small thing to place that much trust in Him and accept that He will guide your behaviors with better wisdom and care than you can do by yourself. Dear child, I know that is hard to accept, and it is hard to ignore. The idea of living a life that could be guided by wisdom, I know it is hard because if you are here, then wisdom is not what has guided your life so far. Please, I do not say that to be cruel. We all have our stupid, stubborn mistakes when we've lost all good sense. That is why wisdom can be such a treasure.

That is why I want to give you one simple pearl of wisdom that I have learned. Do not forget overcoming you is no simple feat. It is a daily thing to surrender to something stronger than yourself. It is not a battle quickly fought but a war to be slowly won. Surrendering to greater wisdom and greater care than you can have for yourself is a frightening thing, but often necessary if you ever hope to achieve more than your past self-destructive ways. Christ said it much more elegantly. 'Then He said to the crowd, 'If any of you wants to be My follower, you must turn from your selfish ways, take up your cross daily, and follow Me.'" (Luke 9:23 NLT)

The decision to better yourself by overcoming you and placing your trust in Him starts by understanding it is a slow fight of surrender. Wisdom takes time. Wisdom is patient. Quitting is rash, and giving up never learns. So, sweet darling, fight the you that you must overcome patiently.

Evermore,

Your Kindred Heart

Chapter Four

To whom it may concern;

Your loneliness is of no importance, you know? In fact, it may be your saving grace. Your loneliness spares you any real disappointment. Only if you had someone who really cared about you can there be disappointment. Oh, you may feel self-loathing, but that's not actually disappointment. That soul-crushing realization that you failed someone who really loved you that's true disappointment, but don't worry about that; you don't have anyone like that. Do you? You are alone and lonely because, well, that is probably for the best.

I am not out to be hurtful if that is what you believe. In fact, friend, I'm trying to reassure you. You have yet to disappoint someone, but you have also yet *to let someone have the opportunity. You will fail them. Probably in magnificent fashion even. Okay, so maybe that was a little spiteful, but it is only the truth. You know, that thing you keep trying to avoid. I think you could have solved a lot of your problems if you would have just been honest with yourself. Then again, that would be admitting that you have yet to care or be cared for enough to matter. Which is really worse, though? Being honest or being careless?*

Is there where I tell you to think about your answer? Not likely, friend. In truth, I don't care. I said it from the start. It is of no importance. I think you should know that that is really all. You won't cross any bridges or even burn them until you decide to build them, and until that day, you can happily stand at the precipice of the chasm of your self-loathing and loneliness, trying to decide if it matters. Until you figure out that answer, it honestly doesn't.

Evermore,
Your Wounded Sensitivities

❋❋❋

After work, Emilia changed her shirt then sat at her small kitchen table waiting for her phone to ring. She had decided not to wait to set up the video visiting system with Misty. She would not lie to herself. She really did not like going into the prison, so although this was not ideal, it was better than the alternative. Now she nervously wondered if Misty really meant for her to do this.

When her phone vibrated, she nearly dropped it in an attempt to answer it. Once she accepted it, Misty's exotic features filled her phone's screen with a small timer counting down thirty minutes in red numerals in the top corner.

Before she caught herself, Emily said, "Even with this video quality, you still look beautiful."

Misty burst into a surprising fit of giggles, "Well, hello to you too, babe. Is that a bit of jealousy I hear?"

Emily grimaced, "Maybe a little."

Misty laughed again, "That's nice to know. I always thought you were the pretty one." Emily rolled her eyes, "It's true, dear. I might have the sexy lips, but you've got the eyes."

"I'm just going to ignore that. This is so weird." She exclaimed.

"It is," Misty agreed, "but I'm glad you decided to do it. I wasn't sure if you would."

Emily pursed her lips before admitting, "I asked my sponsor if it was a good idea first."

"Good for you." Misty responded sincerely, "I'm glad you're taking it seriously. I worried about you. In here, I don't have a choice, but for you, it's different."

"He said something similar. He cautioned me that it could be more dangerous for you because of something like that, but he cautiously encouraged it."

This time Misty rolled her eyes, "Cautiously encouraged it? Sounds like some of the priests that come through here."

"Pastor. A church-sponsored my recovery program."

Misty's beautiful emerald eyes widened, letting the pure green catch the light from somewhere off the camera, "Really? How does that work?"

Emily shrugged, "He just walked into the hospital one day and said if I was serious about it that it was an option. Now that I'm out of the clinic, I have to go see him once a week so he can see that I'm adjusting and dealing in healthy ways, but I'm okay with that."

Misty quirked her lips in a small smile, "That does sound pretty good. I'm a little jealous now. What was your program like?"

"They were big on the group sharing and counseling for one thing." Emily offered dejectedly.

"Yeah, I think that is all of them, but you can't knock results. Did they do the homework assignments thing?"

"Yes! Writing letters to yourself at some future point or to the people you've hurt. Self-assessment surveys of your progress. I don't think I did that much writing in high school."

"Like we could remember if we did." Misty chuckled softly at her attempt of humor, "I know what you mean, though. It did kind of make me wish they still didn't let us have pens."

"You can have pens? I thought that was a safety issue?" Emily asked, genuinely curious.

Misty laughed, truly amused at Emily's cluelessness, "They have what they call prison pens. They are almost entirely rubber and flexible and really short, so there is almost no way to turn them into anything dangerous. Also, they only give us two at a time, and they check to see if we have them periodically, and we have to give the used ones back if we need another one."

"That sounds kind of strict. What do you do if you lose one?"

"You don't lose one." Misty answered seriously.

Emily grimaced, "Sorry, I guess I kind of forgot where you were. It's not a regular clinic."

"No, no, it's not." Misty said with no bitterness in her voice, "But it was good for me. If this was a clinic that I could walk out of, I don't think I would have made it this far. Do you know what I mean?"

"Actually, I don't. It was different for me. When I got to the clinic, the worst of it was over, it felt like."

"How's that?"

"Well, I had spent nearly three days in the hospital restrained to the bed on suicide watch. They gave me something to help the effects of the drugs in my system, but the withdrawal was-"

"Excruciating." Misty finished for her.

"That sounds like a good word. You wonder for the first couple of days if it is worth it to get clean or if it would just be easier to die."

"It has to be worth it." Misty said sternly, "Otherwise, the pain we caused would mean nothing, and maybe you don't carry as much pain as I do, but you carry enough. Don't give up."

"I won't."

"So, what's it like being clean and on the outside?" Misty asked.

"Is that a good idea?" Emily asked hesitantly.

"Letting me live vicariously through you? Why not? Are you doing something you shouldn't?" Misty asked with the smirk on her lips sparkling in her eyes.

"No!" Emily answered, exasperatedly amused, "I just didn't know if that would be good for you. I work in a coffee shop there is no vicarious living to be had. I'm sorry."

"Well, at least you get to meet people." Misty said consolingly.

"Yeah." Emily answered, not realizing she had rolled her eyes.

"Oh, now you definitely need to spill it."

"It's nothing really. Just this guy I met the other day."

"Are you allowed relationships with your recovery program?" Misty asked, slightly surprised.

"No. It is still strongly discouraged until I am in a healthier place," Misty was nodding along knowingly, "but there was just something different about him. I mean, you tell a guy you had a drug problem, and it is completely acceptable that he runs, right?"

"Wait! You told this guy you were a junkie, and he didn't write you off? What kind of damaged goods is he?" Misty asked.

"He's not damaged. He is just actually a nice guy. Sweet, in a way."

"And you didn't jump him right there on the spot." Emily frowned at her, "Sorry, I forgot you were always kind of frigid."

"Ow!" Emily objected.

"Sorry babe. I love you, but you are an ice queen." Misty stopped to look Emily over on the screen, "I never did know why."

"I wasn't an ice queen." Emily objected futilely.

"Whatever, babe. You aren't an ice queen, and I'm not talking to you from a prison visitors' room. The only problem is they just don't make a recovery program for your problem that doesn't involve a bar."

"Cute." Emily remarked, seeing the timer blink that they only had five minutes left.

"I see it, too." Misty said, noticing the way Emily's eyes had shifted in the camera, "Can we do this again?"

"I really want to. Are you good with that?"

"Yes, when do you think it will be?" Misty asked.

"I am going to definitely try for once a week, hopefully, more."

"Does it cost you anything?"

"It actually comes from your commissary fund, but that's alright. You should have plenty. If not, let me know."

"Why so you can keep adding to it with Mr. Damaged Goods' tips?" Misty asked with another smirk.

"Does it really bother you, or did you just want an excuse to call him that?"

Misty shrugged, "I think I mostly just wanted to call him that. I want more details next time." She paused, looking to the corner of her screen again, "Love you, babe."

"Love you too."

The video call terminated before either of them could say anything more. Emily sighed. It had felt good to talk to her friend without being surrounded by prison bars, and she felt that Misty had enjoyed it too, or she would not have asked to do it again. She knew her group would consider part of this as seeking closure, but it was more than that. Misty was her friend, even without the drugs. Misty had been into marijuana in high school, and although Emily was not exactly a straight arrow in school, she never felt pressured to smoke with Misty, and Misty never tried to push it on her. Emily knew it was how she had to cope with her home life. She had grown up with a verbally and emotionally abusive mother and an alcoholic father who just did not care. Even then, Misty was a bright, upbeat girl in Emily's life.

When things took a turn for the worse in Emily's future, it was Misty who was there. By then, Misty had gotten into what the counselors called "hard substances," but she had not pressed Emily into them. It was Emily who had asked for them from Misty, and Misty gave them to her because, after all, what were friends for. Perhaps, that friendship should have at least amounted to Emily being able to suffer the bars and security just to see her friend, but it still made Emily think too much of the clinic and she, although would be thankful for that place, hated it. Instead, she went through the process on her phone to schedule another call for the next week.

***

To My Unkindled Love,

After you accept the slow fight of surrender that will help you to overcome yourself. Next comes the truly hard part. You must take an inventory of what you are fighting and what you have to fight with. You must make a searching and fearless moral inventory of yourself! You must better understand your depths by gently ripping away the many layers of your being. No, that is not some metaphysical quandary, sweet child. It is simply a state of truth. You've heard the Bible stories by now. I am sure of how we are just but filthy rags. It is time to strip them away like the death cloths that were draped upon Lazarus. Strip away your fears, your anxieties, your hatreds, your self-loathing, strip away everything holding you to that death of self, and only then can you find the life that God wishes you to bring up out of that place.

Only then will you allow yourself to experience a much fuller healing, restoration, and freedom. All of this is meant to lead you back to that strong, powerful God that will help you to overcome yourself. Only then, once you have examined yourself honestly and completely, will you be brought up out of that place of every deep, dark, and hateful thing you despise in who you are and who you think you've become. To state it ever so plainly from the source, "Instead, let us test and

examine our ways. Let us turn back to the Lord."
(Lamentations 3:40 NLT)

It is never so easy to look in on one's self. To examine those selfish ways. But only by doing so can one find the wounds and the cancers that need to be healed. Only after knowing the worst parts of yourself will you know what to bring to God in a relationship that will overcome and overwhelm you with healing and restoration. So, sweet darling, let me make sure you read it first here so you can have no qualms later, and I need you to pay close attention, dear child. Turn back! Read the verse again. Let us turn back to the Lord. Know now that you will hear several times that you cannot do it and that you will not make it. Repeatedly, you will hear others around you telling you to turn back, and you will begin to say it yourself. So, when you decide to listen to that. It is okay, sweet child, just when you turn back... turn back to the Lord.

Evermore,
Your Kindred Heart

Chapter Five

To whom it may concern;

The writing comes easier, you know. I know the voices never left, but now I know I am able to transcribe them again. Not that I am sure that I want to be able to read what they have to say, but if I do not allow them this small freedom, I do not think I will ever escape this torment. That is perhaps the real torture, to continually write this only to dredge myself through the pain just to see if I find liberty or enslavement. I get the sentiment now. Give me liberty or give me death, right? The funny thing about that phrase, though, it sounds like they are okay with either not necessarily saying it has to be the one. So, which one do they really want? The liberty? Or just the death, the escape? If one is the goal, then the other is just a crutch, and yet both would be required for the paralyzed and broken to walk again. It is funny how even the necessities can still be crutches.

Maybe, just perhaps, that is only because I am so used to being crippled. It is not a sympathy plea, just a simple fact. Physically, mentally, and emotionally, I am a cripple. The physical, well, who really cares at this point about that? There are routines and remedies for the physically impaired that even if they don't want it or like it, they can still do it. Their bodies can scream and protest all they must, but habits can be formed and forged. That wonderful word, rehabilitation, can be achieved when your brokenness is only physical.

But mentally and emotionally? Those are the tickets. You can go throw the motions, and your mind and heart or even call it your soul does not even have to protest for it not to even work. Rehabilitation is really a dirty word when it comes to the emotional carnage of a ravaged mind. Mental and emotional health both have been thrown in the darkest depths of the abyss at the back edge of my soul, and I live with only the faintest echoes of the sufferings. I am the result of scarring done by the painful memories. After all, is that not what chaos really is? The frantic denial of pain.

And what happens when you accept the pain? Peace? Perhaps. Happiness? Not likely! Perseverance? Cute. Pain begets pain. If nothing else, pain is

Darren Finney

consistent with its promises, and after all, wouldn't I know. Wouldn't you, my chaotic little mess?

Evermore,

The Crippled Echo

***

She watched him through the window. Emily was not a stalker, it was not like that, but she watched him. Harkin had slipped in this morning when Rosie had been working the front counter, and Emily had not realized he was there yet until one of the girls pointed him out. So, now she watched.

Harkin was focused today. Emily could see that, but what really made her wonder about him was where he sat. Harkin was sitting outside at one of the sidewalk tables. He was sitting in an area where she could not have a legitimate work excuse to speak to him. She worried if it was intentional, other than one brief order exchange they had not really spoken since she had kissed him.

Emily untied her apron then looked to Rosie, "Good if I break?"

"It's about time, girl." She replied with a smile.

Emily strode confidently out the door, then right to Harkin's table, "I'm sorry!" she blurted.

- 75 -

Harkin looked up so that Emily went from being able to inspect his closely cropped salt and pepper hair to seeing his tightly groomed and trimmed beard surrounding his slightly confused, deep walnut brown eyes.

"I'm sorry?" He repeated, curiously.

"I didn't mean to do it." She asserted.

"Do what?"

"Kiss you!" She said on the edge of exasperation.

"Oh! Does that kind of thing happen by accident around you a lot?" Harkin asked with a small twitch at the corners of his mouth.

"Are you screwing with me?" She asked dubiously.

Harkin shrugged, then gestured to the other chair at his table, "That doesn't sound like something I would do."

She lowered herself into the chair with a huff, "You're a jerk."

"Now that wasn't very nice."

"Truth hurts." She muttered.

"So, an apology and an insult. How did I ever get so lucky?" Harkin asked.

His disarming smile reminded Emily why she had come out here in the first place, and she silently kicked herself. She started to open her mouth to say something, but he cut her off.

"Don't."

"Don't, what?" She asked.

"Don't go there." He answered.

She sighed, "I think our conversation would go so much further if we spoke more than three words at a time."

Again, he flashed her that same confident and disarming smile, "I imagine so, but they wouldn't be near as fun. However, don't start apologizing again. I did not come out here to avoid you. That is what you thought, isn't it?" She nodded her head, her lips parted in mild surprise, "Thought so, truthfully my reason is much worse than that."

"Is that so?" She prompted.

"Three words," He remarked with a smile, "but, oh yes. I decided the other day that I really like the way the sun shines off your hair."

"Don't go there." She warned.

Harkin shrugged, "Why can't you just say thank you?"

"Seriously?" She asked in response, a hint of anger rising in her voice.

In reply, Harkin took a slow drink of coffee, never taking his eyes off of hers.

"You're really doing this?" She asked.

"Four words. That's progress. Yes, I am. Tell me, how does a pretty girl become a recovering addict." He answered.

"Technically, it was five words. What do you want me to say?" Emily asked.

"Never mind, you're not ready to tell me. I get it. I think we both need to get back to work."

"Don't you dare dismiss me!" Emily said, her voice rising with the anger flushing her cheeks.

"Calm down," Harkin replied in an equally stern voice as he pointed in the window, "I'm not dismissing you, but I think she wants you."

Emily followed his direction to see Rosie beckon her inside exasperatedly.

She looked back to Harkin, "I'm sorry."

"You really need to stop saying that. Can I walk you home when you get off work? Promise I won't let you kiss me accidentally this time."

She rolled her eyes with a smile as she stood to her feet, "Deal."

*＊＊

Emily watched him. Okay, so maybe it was a bit stalkerish. However, she was rewarded whenever she would catch him watching her. He would give her that smile before looking back at his laptop. She was really starting to enjoy that smile, and she really needed to stop, she kept telling herself. Emily could tell all the usual excuses. She could try to tell herself it was harmless, but no matter what she told herself, it all sounded overly familiar. In fact, it all sounded like the things she would tell herself on the real bad days that led to her calling her sponsor. Emily was beginning to wonder if she really should call her sponsor about this, actually.

She had to suppress a small smile when she saw Harkin close his computer and lean back into his chair, looking out over the sunny afternoon like he had not noticed it before. Emily realized he probably really had not noticed the way he would focus on his computer. She would not have been surprised if it had turned dark before he noticed. She sat her apron in the back and said goodnight to the closing shift girls on her way out. She walked over to his table and sat down.

"How's everything in Romance's I.T. department today?" She asked.

"Romance is dead." Harkin replied drearily.

"So, what does that do for your job?" Emily asked casually.

"It'll thrive."

"I don't follow."

"Everyone says they want a love story. Even in the beginning of Creation, God sought to rid perfection of loneliness. Of course, life is not conducive to the same want. Progress and passion rarely walk hand in hand. Once there were days when love's correspondence journeyed with all the frailty of wax and postage glue, then we decided that we could strip away the emotion by the glare of a computer screen and a send button. The mystique of desire has been burned off the idea of the relationship the same way the morning mist is burnt off the lake on a summer morning. All that is left is the sweltering misery and fear of being alone. There is no romance. Just an algorithm to tell people to give it a shot."

Emily sat quietly for a minute, absorbing what Harkin had said before finally saying, "You really don't have a healthy view of your job, but then again, that is probably normal. There is just so much to unpack there. First of all, a God reference? You didn't strike me as the type. Sorry."

"I'm not, but you still pick up a thing or two here or there."

"Fair enough. I guess."

"I take it; you still don't agree." Harkin said with a half-smile, "This is where you tell me you're one of those Jesus-freak types. How does that work with your past again?"

"That's a bit harsh!" Emily exclaimed, feigning offense, "But I get it. I imagine for someone like you, it doesn't make sense. My past is why I do believe in hope."

"Hope?" Harkin repeated incredulously.

"Yes! Hope!" Emily said, exasperated, "Are you telling me that you don't even have the thought that things could be better than you cling to that hope?"

Harkin spared her a sideways glance but did not respond.

"If it wasn't for hope, I'd still be an addict." Emily asserted, "but why do you do this job if you apparently hate what it represents?" Emily asked, standing to her feet and motioning for him to follow her.

"It's what I'm good at. I got started doing something similar creating census pools and algorithms for different projects in college. A professor of mine knew a guy, and at first, I worked for only one company. Then I got a lot of what I did declare proprietary and was able to use that to work freelance for multiple companies." Harkin paused, looking around the sidewalk, "I thought you lived the other way?"

"I thought we'd take the long way around. Give us a chance to talk." Harkin arched an eyebrow at her, "I mean, come on. I don't even really know anything about you." Emily insisted.

"What's there to know?" Harkin offered with a shrug.

"That's how you want to play this? Fine. We'll start with something simple. What was the real reason for the suit?"

"I was visiting my sister."

"What? Is she just a stickler for dress code?"

"She's dead." Harkin answered.

Emily stopped walking and looked at his back as he kept his stride.

"I'm sorry." She said.

"You didn't kill her." Harkin stated as he turned to face her on the sidewalk.

"Why do you visit her?" She asked as she joined him again.

"It was her birthday and because her parents won't."

"Her parents? Aren't they your parents too?" She questioned, turning to look at him.

This time, it was Harkin who stopped. There was a chilling sensation that started at the small of her back and crawled icily up her spine when Emily met his eyes. For a man that radiated warmth, Emily could see that in him was nothing but hard ice. Emily was not worried for her safety, but she recognized that emotionally Harkin was as dangerous as the sun being reflected off a frozen lake.

"The one thing I am grateful for is that she died before they had a chance to fail her."

Harkin turned to keep walking, but Emily grabbed his arm to stop him. She did not say anything but peered deep into that intense cold that was burning beneath the surface. In truth, she was beginning to fear the idea of breaking through the ice and being plunged into those depths.

"She died. They quit." Harkin spat out almost defensively, "I was hurting too, and I kept going. They just checked out and stopped being parents."

"How old were you? How old was she?"

Harkin shrugged, "I was sixteen. She was thirteen."

Emily nodded slowly, "And how old are you now?"

Harkin flashed a remnant of the good-humored smile she had seen so often before turning to walk again and asking, "What's your guess?"

"Nope," She said, shaking her head playfully, "I'm not stepping into that trap. I mean, if we were talking about how old you acted, I might go as high as five, but I am not answering based on looks."

Harkin grimaced, "I look that rough, huh?" Emily arched an eyebrow in a warning, and he relented, "Fine, I'm thirty-six."

Harkin noticed she did a remarkable job of not reacting to the number.

"So, for twenty years, you've carried this... what would you call it?" Emily asked.

"Nope, I'm not stepping into that trap." he replied.

"See!" Exclaimed, "So, you know this isn't healthy."

Harkin sighed, "There's no way for me to win here, is there?"

"Excuse me," Emily said with a flourish to herself, "You are debating with a pretty girl. The odds were never in your favor."

"Hmm, I don't remember saying pretty."

"How nice! It was inferred. But seriously, you've carried this around for twenty years. You say they checked out, but what about you?"

"What about me?" Harkin asked defensively.

"Are you going to say you didn't check out?"

"I didn't."

"Really? Who was the last person who was real?"

Harkin stopped, "I believe this is your door. Have a good evening."

He turned to leave, and Emily reached out to grab his arm this time. Too late, she realized that she was upset as she felt her nails digging into his skin.

"Hey!" The volume in her voice surprised her, "I told you! Don't you dare dismiss me!"

Emily watched Harkin's jaw clench either in anger or biting off a retort, maybe both. That was when it happened. She let go of his arm to draw back and slap him across the face.

"Feel better?" He asked, the frozen depths of his soul showing on his features and spilling harshly into his voice.

She pulled back to hit him again, but he caught her wrist. He pulled her not roughly but firmly so that she lost her balance. She fell against him, her back against his chest, then he wrapped his arms around her, pinning hers to her chest.

"Sorry, you only get one for free." Harkin whispered in her ear, the coldness in his voice slowly ebbing away.

"Let me go!" She breathed as she squirmed against him.

"When you promise to stop hitting me." He said, a warmth returning to his voice, and she realized he was trying not to laugh.

Emily relaxed against him, letting her anger dissolve. She realized she felt comfortable in his arms, and that made her uneasy. Harkin spoke softly from behind her as he let her go then stepped back, and she wondered if he had felt the same thing.

"You're right. Nora was the last person that was real to me, but that does not mean I checked out. That I gave up."

"Some addicts close down when they sober up. They worry about feeling something that they can crave like a drug. They're afraid that they are just going to end up replacing one vice for another. So, really, they just stop living. They lose hope."

"And we're back to that." Harkin dismayingly remarked.

"Yes! I know how it sounds, but I know what it's like to live without hope, and yeah, sure, you may not be looking to a chemical hope, but that's only because you like being bitter. It's your drug." Emily said, finally turning to look into his eyes.

Harkin's voice sounded distant as he said, "I'm not you."

Emily sneered, "I know. I at least admitted I have a problem."

"I'm sorry." Harkin said as she reached for her door, "I shouldn't have said that."

"You don't get to skip to step nine until you get past the first one." She said before closing the door on him.

✱✱✱

To My Unkindled Love,

Now that you've more closely examined yourself, more closely examined the darkness that you find in yourself, you must gather your courage and confess! Not just to yourself, but to others and to God. You admit to God, to yourself, and to another human being the exact nature of your wrongs. By admitting what you've previously been hiding, you can better accept yourself and make changes in your relationships. I understand the fear that your examination inspires. Even worse, I understand your hesitancy at the idea of being so intimately connected to somebody as to have no secrets before them. Whether that be God or someone you are even afraid to even call a friend.

That intimate connection is part of the healing, and, sweet darling, you need healing. But it comes from confession. You've heard the verse by now, I'm sure. "Confess your sins to each other and pray for each other so that you may be healed. The earnest prayer of a righteous person has great power and produces wonderful results." (James 5:16 NLT)

It may sound counter-intuitive to spend so much energy turning to God only to then rely on another person as well to overcome you. That is why words like accountability and support are used to hide the true feeling of it. There will always be moments of guilt and shame in the slow fight to overcome yourself. That is why you need others. Somebody else will have to be willing to fight for you when you do not think you can keep fighting. It takes courage and endurance to confess the you that you must overcome. It takes more than just you to carry that to God.

Evermore,

Your Kindred Heart

Chapter Six

To whom it may concern;

Let's be clear about something; sticking your fingers in the barrel of a loaded gun then pulling the trigger to see if the safety is working does not indicate a problem with the safety! Just as telling lies because the truth is hard doesn't make it any easier. Oh, I know how easy it is to get lost in fiction, and there is nothing wrong with that, but you are talking about fantasy here. The fantasy that you can live that lie so well that it could become your reality, that it could become your life. That fantasy, that pipedream so aptly called, is you sticking your fingers in the barrel and pulling the trigger. But, know this, fiction is your safety.

Fiction is the birthplace of dreams. It is the subconscious thought that it will make a good story to tell the grandkids. Love, ambition, success, and every good thing that triggers your anxiety... it's all fiction, in the sense that someone thought it would be a story for the ages.

Your problem and mine, friend, is that we are far too content to transcribe the story and much too afraid to make a story of our own. The truth of it is, you like all the pretty words, not their meaning, because if something has meaning, it's REAL, and you won't be able to hide behind the fiction anymore. Perhaps, if you're so content to flick that safety and pull the trigger, then maybe you should load the gun properly and do this right. Put some meaning in it! Make it real!

Evermore,

The Meaningless Writer

❋❋❋

It is about more than a good bedside manner. There is the darker side of the job that, in time, becomes the hated and dreaded side of the job. Klarissa hated being an angel of death. That is what they called it anyway. It was at least one of the nicer terms she had heard. It had started as being a home healthcare nurse, mostly coming to check or administer medications, checking machines, or helping dialysis patients. Now, Klarissa mostly sat at the bedsides of hospice patients, helping to keep them comfortable and to keep an eye on the well-being of the family.

Klarissa had never realized how much work that the last one could be. With her current patient, half of her check-in meant asking his wife if she was eating or, as the case was today, sending her to shower and change her clothes because she had not done either since Klarissa's last visit.

Her patient looked away from the window to watch her as she was adjusting the dialysis machine. It never failed with some of them that even on their death bed, they leered at the pretty young nurse, but she could tell by his gaze that was not why he was looking at her.

"Do you get tired of watching people die?" His voice was beginning to show the signs of his body's strain and starting to fade, but it held no bitterness in it.

'I prefer to think that I'm keeping you comfortable." Klarissa replied.

"Because my comfort level is so important." He said with a haggard laugh.

"It's all we can do." Klarissa admitted.

"That is due to no choice of your own. I couldn't do your job."

"It's not all bad days." Klarissa said absent-mindedly. The way she always did in these kinds of conversations.

"I would hate to think what you call a good time. So, that's the machine that's dragging this out?"

"Dragging this out?" She repeated.

"I'm going to die. It is only a matter of when I've accepted that, and I would drink to it if such a thing were allowed. What happens when that machine gets turned off?"

"For the time being, it won't." Klarissa said flatly.

"Humor an old man."

"Your body would go into septic shock, and you would die within forty-eight hours, but it's not a good way to go."

"Isn't that how it going to happen anyway?" Her patient asked matter-of-factly.

"Eventually, yes, your sepsis will spread and continue to spread throughout your body faster than this machine can clean your blood, but it could be gradual. Shutting off the machine, it would be all at once and painful. Also, this way, you have time to say your goodbyes. Not everyone gets that, although a lot of them would like that opportunity."

"Young lady, I wish that opportunity hadn't been wasted on me."

"Everybody wants to say goodbye." Klarissa admonished.

"You may be right. My hands aren't working too well anymore. Would you be willing to write something down for me?"

"Of course, sir."

"Grab that pen and pad over there. I'll tell you what to write."

***

"She doesn't want to come out here." The barista said as she cleaned the sidewalk table next to Harkin.

He had been staring pointlessly at his computer screen for the last ten minutes or so and had not realized she had been talking to him until she stepped over to his table.

"I bed your pardon." Harkin said, looking up at her.

"Emily doesn't want to come out here and talk to you." The barista clarified.

"That's alright, ma'am. I definitely deserve that. That's why I sat out here, so she wouldn't have to."

"It's Rosie, not ma'am. What did you do anyway?" Rosie asked, eying him speculatively.

Harkin sighed, "Said something I shouldn't have."

There was a spark of disapproving interest in Rosie's eyes when she said, "I really think you should find another place to drink coffee and work."

Harkin reached up to close his laptop when another voice said, "No, it's fine."

Harkin looked up to see Emily standing on the sidewalk now. She looked to Rosie apologetically.

"I'm sorry. Can we have a minute?" Emily asked.

"Of course, sweetie." She shot Harkin another disapproving look, who sensed her almost motherly protectiveness of Emily, before turning to face Emily directly, "I say this solely as your friend and not your boss, but I don't think he should keep coming around."

"And as my boss?" Emily asked nervously.

For the first time, Harkin saw Rosie smile as she spoke, "You're a hard worker, and I know he won't ever be worth firing you over. You have nothing to worry about. Enjoy your break and be back on time."

Emily sat down across from Harkin after Rosie walked away, then crossed her arms, looking at him expectantly.

Harkin sighed, "It wasn't fair to say that. To throw your past in your face like that."

"I said I didn't want you to apologize." Emily interrupted before he had a chance to continue like he clearly was planning to.

"I wasn't." Emily arched an eyebrow at him, "Let me finish. You were right. I have a problem with addiction. I am addicted to my bitterness."

Emily smirked at him, "I like the way that sounds. Very clever, considering. Also, that was big of you."

"I'm trying. There is a part of me that wants to just accuse you of being addicted to hope, but I know that would be-"

"Rude?" Emily suggested.

Harkin shrugged, "Among other things. I really am trying here."

"You said that already."

"Did they make it this hard for you when you did this?" Harkin asked defensively.

Emily leaned forward, resting her folded arms on the table, her blue eyes piercing him, "Actually, they kept me restrained to the hospital bed to make sure I didn't hurt myself while I went through withdrawal after nearly overdosing."

"I'm sorry."

"I will accept that apology. I'm told it is only natural to want to lash out at this point."

"Don't do that." Harkin said calmly, but Emily heard the chill edging into his voice.

Emily waved a hand to dismiss it, "I have to go back to work. Do you want to walk me home today?"

"I'm sorry, I'm not staying today. I just wanted to come and tell you that you were right. Do you work tomorrow?"

"No, it's a Sunday." When Harkin shrugged, she rolled her eyes, "How about this? Meet me here at nine-thirty tomorrow morning and come to church with me." Harkin started to object, but she cut him off again, "You want to call it an addiction, then you should at least attempt to understand it before you judge it."

"Okay," He relinquished, "I'll be here tomorrow morning. Get back to work before she changes her mind about me being worth getting you in trouble." Harkin said with a smile.

***

Pastor Ray sat behind his desk reading when Emily walked in. He casually closed the book and smiled up at her.

"Ah, Emily! I'll admit I was surprised to get your call. Is everything alright?"

"Yes. Am I interrupting?"

"Not at all, dear. Please come in, have a seat, and tell me what's on your mind."

Emily sat down in a chair and began playing with her nails.

"Miss Nichols?" Ray softly prompted, "I can wait all night, but it will be easier on you if you tell me sooner."

"What is faith?" Emily asked.

"The substance of things hoped for, the evidence of things not seen. According to Hebrews 11:1, but something tells me that is not the answer you are looking for right now."

"Is faith an addiction to hope?" Emily asked.

Pastor Ray sighed, then he did something Emily had not seen him do before. He rubbed his eyes wearily.

"I personally would refrain from using the word addiction given your previous lifestyle. For you, that word is going to carry some very serious negative connotations. That is, of course, understandable, but there is a different side to addiction."

"Like what?"

"Your experience with addiction was centered around cravings and compulsions. Right now, that is what you are trying to reconcile with your understanding of faith, isn't it?"

"Yes." Emily admitted.

Ray nodded, "That's why it worries you?"

"Yes." Emily admitted, again.

"Don't let it. Addiction is not just a compulsion. It is a dependency, and dependency can be healthy. For example, faith is a dependence on God even when things get hard. Belief is a dependence on hope. Accountability is a dependence on the strength of others when you feel weak. So, yes, if you want to put it crudely, faith and hope are both addictions, but if you want to look at it honestly, they are a dependency on God."

"So, it's not the same thing as trading one vice for another?"

"Of course not! You removed a craving by developing a dependency."

"I know to you that may sound different, but to me, it sounds like you are splitting hairs." Emily confessed.

"A craving means you are hungry for something you don't have. A dependency is a reliance on something you already have. You have removed that part of you that was searching for a way to fill the emptiness and instead have found a hope that you rely on and can build from. Tell me what brought this about?" Pastor Ray asked, giving her a curious look.

"The guy I told you about last time, we were talking and..." Emily trailed off, looking at her nails again.

"And he called your hope an addiction? Not a very chivalrous thing to do."

"I had accused him of being addicted to bitterness, so I think I kind of had it coming." Emily confessed with an embarrassed grimace.

Pastor Ray frowned, "I'm not sure how I feel about you developing this friendship." He held up his hand at the affronted look on her face, "This isn't just because of your recovery. This gentleman does not sound like he is in a healthy lifestyle himself, and this could be destructive to either of you."

"What if you had a chance to meet him? Would you still feel that way?" She saw the spark of interest in his eyes, then she said, "He's agreed to come tomorrow."

His frown returned, "I will never turn anyone away from these doors, but I'm still saying proceed carefully."

***

Harkin settled himself on the ground after tracing his fingers across Nora's name.

"Hi, sis." Harkin sighed, "You look beautiful today." Harkin paused, listening to the slow shuffle coming up behind him, "Hello, Benji."

"Harry. Your visits normally aren't so close together." Benjamin said, easing himself down next to Harkin, "I'm sorry, but that worries an old man like me."

"Benji, you've been doing this as long as I've known you. Been here before my time, so can I ask you something?"

"Of course."

"Everyone you've seen come through here. How many of them hold on to their bitterness?"

"Harry, I don't want to speak out of turn."

Harkin chuckled, "I guess that answers my next question, too. Don't worry, Benji. I was told that I'm addicted to bitterness already."

"Well, that makes me side of the conversation a lot easier." Benjamin said, laughing.

"So, you agree with that?" Harkin asked with more curiosity than resentment.

"I'm no expert on addiction, but you, young man? I don't think you would know what to do without your bitterness, but I don't think you are unique to that. This is where hope is laid to rest and bitterness is born."

"For a gravedigger, you can be awfully poetic sometimes."

"Sidestep it if you want, but that does not change the truth." Benjamin responded.

"Would you just tell me the truth of it, then?"

Benjamin turned to look him over before answering. When he spoke, Harkin could tell he had weighed every word several times.

"It is no light thing, the truth. It has a way of putting a burden on a man's mind, chains on his heart, and a little tarnish on his soul. Are you sure you want that?"

"I'm not sure I have a choice anymore, do I? If that is what truth can do are you telling me that bitterness is any better?" Harkin asked in the way of reply.

Benjamin smiled, "Sometimes, you surprise me, but enough procrastinating. You embraced bitterness when you prepared to place that little girl in the ground. You filled a grave and left yourself empty. Now, I know people like to say all that crap about how time heals everything, and some of them even like to believe it, but it's a useless sentiment to most. Time does nothing but magnifies the situation, and your situation is that little girl is gone."

"Again, I'm not saying I know anything about addiction," Benjamin continued, "but you certainly made a best friend out of that emptiness you carry. You could have had a nice life, you know, done the whole wife and kids thing yourself instead of making a mockery of it with your math problems. Maybe you could have even made a friend or two. You'd just rather be mad at the world and use this little girl as the reason, and that isn't fair to her."

"What do you think I should do?" Harkin asked.

"For starters, I think it's about time you let her go and live your own life. Then maybe you should see about giving a little forgiveness to the ones you still hate for this; I know you drive by their place every time to get here."

"Is that all?"

"No. Whoever told you that you were addicted to bitterness, maybe you should start listening to them.

They might be on to something. I know you hate to hear it, but maybe God's got a plan after all."

Harkin sighed, "You know, I don't believe in all that."

"And you know that I do." Benjamin replied calmly.

"You believe everybody deserves forgiveness no matter what they did?" Harkin asked.

"Myself? I would like to amend that too if they were truly sorry, but yes, I believe everyone deserves forgiveness even when it's hard."

"Why?"

Benjamin shrugged, "Maybe, I'm just tired of burying grudges. I don't know."

"Is it really that easy for you to boil it all down to that? I mean, I've seen that book you all carry."

Benjamin smirked, "Perhaps if you came inside once or twice, it would help."

"I'm about to make that mistake, too." Harkin said miserably.

Benjamin eyed him speculatively until Harkin elaborated.

"I agreed to go with someone to church tomorrow."

"I'll be praying for them." Benjamin said with a smile.

"I get that is something you people say, but why do I feel like I've been insulted?" Harkin asked.

In response, Benjamin just laughed as he stood to his feet.

He stood there a moment before saying, "You'd be doing a good thing to go. Not just to church tomorrow and not just to see your parents, but from here too. Now I've enjoyed your company, but I wouldn't take offense if I didn't see you so often."

Harkin held out his hand, and Benjamin pulled him to his feet. They both stood there for a moment in silence, looking at Nora's headstone.

Harkin finally said in a low voice, "You might be right. Benji. So long."

"So long, Mr. Lindsey." Benjamin replied, shaking hands with Harkin.

✱✱✱

There is something to be said for a man when he has been made uncomfortable, Emilia thought. She stood on the sidewalk watching as Harkin walked up to her. She had been watching him walk toward her for two blocks, and in all fairness, she knew he had been watching her. Maybe, she told herself again, that was why she had made no attempt to move any closer to him. Emily had stood in the same spot wearing her best smile, watching him walk toward her. With each step Harkin took, she could clearly see an awkward anxiousness building in him, and she would have been lying if she had said she did not relish it just a little. Emilia was not cruel, but after all his usual smug confidence, it was amusing to see him squirm just a little.

When he stopped in front of her, Emily saw the briefest hint of a smile, but mostly she could see what really resembled dread. Okay, she admitted to herself, part of her was enjoying this way more than it should have. It was that part of her that spoke next.

"How do I look?" She asked with a small flourish of her dress.

Emily was wearing a blue cotton summer dress that Rosie had bought for her to wear to church, saying it would really go good with her eyes. It was a casual, sleeveless dress with a sporty look. Emily thought the high round neckline and slightly flared skirt were comfortable and yet modest enough to wear to church without drawing dirty looks.

"I'd say heavenly but considering our destination, that might be inappropriate." Harkin answered, a hint of his usual confidence returning.

She rolled her eyes and gestured to her dress, "I was serious."

"So was I, but if it helps, it was a beautiful dress that you have made extraordinary."

Emily rolled her eyes again, "Is this insufferable hopelessness of yours a nerves thing, or is there an off switch somewhere?"

This time, Harkin's smile broke all the way through the dread as he laughed, "I'll never tell."

"Don't be so sure." She warned with a glare as she turned and beckoned with her finger for him to follow. When he fell into step beside her, she said, "You look nice, by the way."

Harkin looked down at his suit then adjusted his tip clip self-consciously. It was a black, off-the-rack number that he had bought two years ago when he had to meet with one of the boards for the company he was freelancing with.

"I've heard people talk about their Sunday best. This was the best I could do."

A smile played across Emily's lips as she said, "Considering where we're going, that's rather appropriate."

"How's that?" Harkin asked.

"Have you really never been to church?"

"No, but I get the gist of it." Harkin answered with a shrug.

Emily was shaking her head, "Apparently not. All anyone can ever bring into a church is the best they can do. Even though it's not enough or falls short, as the church type like to say, it's all they've got. You asked me how my belief works with my past. This is how by knowing a screw-up like me is still welcome."

Harkin was frowning at her when she finished, but he did not say anything. After walking another two blocks in silence and him still wearing that frown, she decided he had sulked long enough.

"What?" She asked a little testily.

"I don't think you get to call yourself a screw-up anymore." She looked over at him as she faltered a step, and he continued, "I'm just saying, you seem to be figuring it all out again. You might have made a mistake, but that doesn't make you a screw-up."

"Thank you." She said, feeling the heat flush her cheeks.

Harkin shrugged again, "It's the truth."

She was still staring at him, so awestruck by his words that she almost let them walk by the turn to the church. She grabbed his arm without thinking, and he lost his balance mid-step. The shift caused Emily to fall back against the building they were walking next to. Harkin caught himself with his off foot and a hand against the wall above her. She felt her back against the brick façade and his body against hers. It was not a painful weight, but it left them standing close enough to one another that they could feel each other's breath on their lips. Emily froze, watching his eyes focus on hers, then drift down to her lips before slowly meeting her eyes again.

"Sorry," Emily whispered, "we needed to go this way."

For a moment, she was not sure that Harkin had heard her. He kept staring into her eyes, his breathing slow and calm, and his body still holding hers in place. Emily was not sure what she wanted him to do, acknowledge that she had said something or just kiss her, but she understood, maybe hoped, that he was having the same debate. When he blinked, it was as if the spell broke. Harkin stepped back wordlessly and made a small flourish of his hand, indicating for her to lead the way.

She stepped away from the building and began to walk again, waiting for him to fall into step. When he did, she could feel that something was different. She turned her head to say something but closed her mouth before any words came. If he noticed, Harkin did not say anything. After a few more steps, she tried again, and her voice did not fail her this time.

"I'm sorry, Harkin."

"You keep saying that." He remarked without looking at her.

"I know. I don't think we can be just friends, can we?"

There was a sad smile in Harkin's eyes when he answered, "We have to be, don't we?"

They stepped into the church's yard before Emily could respond, and the answers in her mind crushed her, but she told herself to just keep going. He was still there after all.

✳✳✳

Walking into the church, Harkin felt his nerves beginning to fray again, and the longer he was there, the worse it seemed to get. He was watching Emily, the way she laughed and smiled when she talked with everyone there or the way the little ones came up to hug her, and he was captivated by the way her smile changed when she talked to the kids. It was the way that it reached her eyes then, he realized. He had chosen to stay back by the entrance while she went around greeting everyone, and occasionally she would look up to let their eyes meet, and her eyes would still have that shine in them from her smile, and she could see that he could not take his eyes off her.

He wondered how obvious it was to everybody else. It was the question that made him jump at the hand on his shoulder. Harkin turned to see an older gentleman comfortably dressed in a much better fitting suit than Harkin's.

"Hello there, son. You look like a new face here." The man said, holding out his hand to shake Harkin's.

"Just passing through." Harkin replied politely as they shook.

"Ah, I see. My name is Raymond Scott, but everybody just calls me Pastor Ray or Ray for short." Pastor Ray said with a friendly smile.

"Harkin Lindsey, but just call me Harry."

"Well, Harry, if you don't mind my asking, what brings you to our little church?" Pastor Ray asked politely.

As Harkin began to stammer out an answer, Emily returned and threw her arms around the pastor, saying, "Good morning, Pastor Ray. This is Harkin, the young man I was telling you about."

"Ah, I see." Pastor Ray said jubilantly and hiding all other reactions, Harkin thought.

"She doesn't call me a young man when the two of you talk, does she?" Harkin asked with a modest smile.

Emily quirked her head at Harkin's attempt at a joke with mild amusement. If she were honest, she had not expected that.

"No, I think that is mostly my doing." Ray answered with a laugh, as another familiar woman came up to his side, "ah, this is my lovely wife-"

"Miss Rosie." Harkin said politely, holding out his hand, intending to shake hers.

Harkin saw the quirk of Emily's lips at his surprise and recovery, but it was an almost approving smile that Rosie gave him as she shook his hand.

"Harkin." She said, her voice void of any affection but also of any malice.

Before anything else could be said, music started playing from the front of the church, and Emily started pulling Harkin to a pew to sit down. Harkin would like to claim that he paid attention, but the only thing he really noticed was the self-conscious way that Emily kept watching him out of the corner of her eye until Pastor Ray stood behind the pulpit with his Bible. In that moment, Emily seemed to sit more attentive, and Harkin understood. There was something about the man that, just before he spoke, seemed to demand everyone's attention.

"There is a safe conversation topic that everybody loves to use. Don't know a person that well. It is a good icebreaker. Don't like a person that much. It keeps it civil. Need to talk about something more serious but not sure how to start. It is a great place to start. You don't want the person to know which category they fall into; they won't do it from this topic." Ray paused to let the polite laughter in the church ring out, and Harkin noticed Emily's little quirk of the lips at the joke before Ray continued speaking, "The topic I am talking about is the weather. We use it all the time! We talk about how the weatherman got it wrong this time. We compare how winters come later and last longer. We love how nice the summer feels and worry how hot it's going to get. Farmers discuss the last frost and first freeze. Even first responders express their concern about fire hazards in a drought. Everyone talks about precautions when it's tornado, hurricane, or flood season."

Ray paused again as he walked around the pulpit to the edge of the dais. The dais was raised six steps above the congregation, and Ray carried his Bible to the top step and sat down to look at the church. From this new position, he was still slightly above everyone's eye level.

"In all these discussions, the weather no one wants to talk about; however, is the weather in their soul—the storm raging in their heart. Everyone chooses to suffer that silently, and the longer the storm goes on, we know what happens. 'Since neither sun nor stars appeared for many days, and no small storm was assailing us, from then on all hope of being saved was gradually abandoned." (Acts 27:20 NASB) The longer we stay in the storm, the harder it is to hold on to hope. Eventually, all those clouds in your mind darken the skies of your thoughts, and you lose your way. Just like these men, they could not plot where they were at. They were well and truly lost and had been for many days. They didn't know where they were going, and they couldn't go back. When that storm rages, it's understandable that you are going to lose your way, and your hope is going to falter." Ray paused to let his eyes scan the faces of the church.

As the pastor's eyes swept the church, Harkin thought he felt the tension building and he was only certain of it when he felt Emily tremble next to him as Ray's eyes swept and seemed to linger over them.

"It is only natural to think that sometimes you need to see the stars in order to plot your course. I don't just mean that literally, either. Some of us have made our jobs or careers and the advancement therein the stars by which we plot our lives. Some have made the relationships we have or the ones we want the stars to plot the way we think we need to live. Some of us have made our pasts, our mistakes, our failures, and our successes the stars by which we plot our future. However, we often forget the all the stars are God-given, and He doesn't need them to see you through. And I know what you are thinking," Ray said, his voice taking on a gravelly accusatory tone, "it is so easy to say that on the clear nights in your lives when you can see the stars so plainly, but when the storm rages on, and you haven't seen the stars in days, it's a little harder to believe that God still sees you through."

Pastor Ray's voice jumped in volume as he exploded with his next words to catch everyone's attention, "But, hey! At least it's not going to kill you. What if that was the sole comfort to what was about to happen in your life? Would you be scared? Or terrified? Worried? Thankful? Would that be enough to give you hope?" His eyes narrowed as he did another sweep of the church, reading the conviction on everyone's face before he continued, "When you feel the weather changing, and you are facing the storm coming in, being told that it won't kill you, that you will see the sun again, will you thank God for that? Seriously, He could have brought you through the storm a million different ways, but that's the way He chooses. How many times do you thank God for the way He brought you through what you've been through?"

Ray stood up and walked back behind the pulpit in silence, letting everyone think about their answers to themselves before he continued saying, "Sometimes you have that storm warning, and you can hunker down in that shelter and pray until it all blows over, sometimes the storm hits without warning, and your life is left looking like a trailer park in tornado alley, and sometimes you have to board up the windows and evacuate until the storm is over. But no matter the way the storm comes, God will see you through, and you will survive. It may not feel like it at first; it rarely does. The men I told you about in verse 20 that were slowly losing hope. They had already been told they would die back in verse 10, "and said to them, 'Men, I perceive that the voyage will certainly be with damage and great loss, not only of the cargo and the ship, but also of our lives.'" (Acts 27:10 NASB) and sure enough, in verses 18 and 19 they began getting rid of the cargo and ship's tackle. It is in that moment when things take a turn. Paul was visited by an angel telling him that the ship he was on would be destroyed, but nobody would die. When he told the crew, he added one more detail, "25Therefore, keep up your courage, men, for I believe

God that it will turn out exactly as I have been told. ₂₆But we must run aground on a certain island." (Acts 27:25-26 NASB) To get through the storm, these men would be shipwrecked. Any of you ever been shipwrecked in your life before?"

Harkin was certain he felt Ray's eyes on him when he asked that question, and he was not certain whether it was Emily or himself that had squirmed at it.

"So, don't believe for a second that when your storm is raging inside of you," Ray continued, "when it feels like too much, when you think it's getting worse, that it's beyond God's plan. Sometimes, the storm is just to strip away the things you don't need but be careful that you don't give up or let fear or worry win. 'Until the day was about to dawn, Paul was encouraging them all to take some food, saying, 'Today is the fourteenth day that you have been constantly watching and going without eating, having taken nothing. ₃₄ Therefore I encourage you to take some food, for this is for your preservation, for not a hair from the head of any of you will perish.' (Acts 27:33-34 NASB) No matter the storm, do not forget to care for yourself, but even then, do not forget it is a temporary thing. 'When they had eaten enough, they began to lighten the ship by throwing out the wheat into the sea.'" (Acts 27:38 NASB)

Again, Ray let the congregation observe these words as he walked down the steps of the dais to stand with them all and continued speaking from there, "To end this story, in verse 44, everyone survives. Whether they swam to the island or had to drift on broken pieces of the ship to get there. God doesn't just trash the ship. He has a plan. I don't know if you're weathering through your own storm today; If you've started to jettison everything from your life in an attempt to just make it through, and I don't know if you've been so focused on the storm that you've stopped taking care of yourself. What I do know is, it's time to let the ship get wrecked so you can make it to the island, and I know for a lot of you that the island isn't where you wanted to go. That's alright! It's where God intended you to be, and that's good enough. See, you're stuck in your storm because you are still worried about YOUR destination, not the safe harbor God has planned. It's okay to lose some things. Some of us need to lose a lot of things, but God reassured Paul to have the courage they wouldn't lose their lives. Just as Jesus reassured us that whosoever believes will have eternal life. Don't let the storm steal your hope just because it can't steal your life. Don't think the island wasn't meant to be. There are a million other ways God could have pulled you from your situation, but the shipwreck and the island are the ones He chooses. Be grateful! He still sees you through. Let us pray."

Harkin bowed his head with the rest of the congregation, and when they said 'amen,' he raised it to see that Emily was not beside him anymore. He quickly scanned to see that she was not in the church at all, but sitting when she had been was a church bulletin with the word "sorry" and a phone number written on it. Harkin stood with everyone else to shake Ray's hand on the way out the door.

When Ray shook Harkin's hand, he leaned forward and whispered, "It's okay, Harry. She slipped out during the prayer because she didn't want to talk to me. It had nothing to do with you."

❋❋❋

To My Unkindled Love,

You should know what lies at the end of that test of endurance. You should know what happens when you can finally confess the you that you need to overcome. You should know that the victory doesn't start there, that your fight doesn't end there. No, by working through your fears and uncertainties about becoming a better person and making the changes you need to make in your life, you prepare yourself to invite God to change you.

That will bring you to the end of the test of your endurance. Know this, my dear one, that is the easy test. Next lies before you, the test of faith. That one is hard. That test requires you to crucify yourself every day and not in the way that you are used to doing already. There is a subtle difference. "Humble yourselves before

Faithfully Addicted

the Lord, and He will lift you up in honor." (James 4:10
NLT) Did you catch it, my sweet darling? Let me lovely
explain.

But, first, do not let the word "humble" distract,
confuse, or comfort you. That word is the very real test
of all of your emotional and spiritual stamina and
endurance, but if you can do it if you can embrace the
test of faith. He will lift you above all of your guilt,
shame, and regret. He will lift you up in honor. That is a
new word, a new sensation for you, but you must be
entirely ready to have God remove all of those defects
of character. You will be able to stop crucifying yourself
on every cross of self-loathing you can build, and you
will be able to crucify yourself on a cross of love that
God will you upon in honor.

Evermore,
Your Kindred Heart

Chapter Seven

To whom it may concern;

Your persistence to believe that cashing in all your lucky stars will pay for all of your dreams is endearing. Endearing but annoying. Don't get excited. This isn't one of those "you've got to make your own way" or "pull yourself up by your bootstraps" pep talks either. This is simply me telling you to give it up and pack it in. Pray tell, given your life so far, how could you possibly believe that you have any lucky stars to cash in? Don't think of me as harsh. That is merely the truth. After all, even in sorrow's marriage of happiness, despair was still made a mistress, and nobody won in that twisted little triangle. No one gets happiness without pain.

Need a better reminder of that? You remember that old story about the man who flew too close to the sun? Icarus was the name, I believe. A man so enraptured by the sensations of flight that he gave way to reckless abandon in the pursuit of happiness and rather fell into the sea where he drowned. I doubt I need to explain the merits of highs and crashes. Take it as a lesson. A person's happiest moment usually is followed by their worst moments. Don't believe that your endeavor will end any differently.

For all you already know, friend. You're already drowning, and you just don't have the good sense to break the surface and breathe. It's called an Icarus moment. Let your wings burn. Your flight is over. Don't believe for a moment you can fly anymore. This is all about sticking the landing. Will you learn to swim or drown?

Evermore,

Destiny's Fated Fool

***

Rosie looked over the top of her book as her husband came in the front door that afternoon. She enjoyed having an actual book. She knew that it was almost old-fashioned these days to read from something that did not have a screen, but she had decided that nothing could beat the feel of a book. There was something about the way the old crisp pages felt and that small swish of noise when she turned one. Also, when it came to the computer screens, she could not slam them shut and thump them down with the same auditory satisfaction that always got her husband's attention.

Rosie Scott had been a pastor's wife for twenty-three years and had been Ray's wife for twenty-seven, and one thing she had learned in that time was how to get his attention. Ray was not a neglectful husband. In fact, sometimes, he could be doting to the point of annoyance, and Rosie had learned to love that too. Ray's problem was that he knew how to deal with too many problems. He handled matters of the church both as a whole and on individual levels so naturally that most times, he did not need to include Rosie in the decisions. Most of the time, he would tell her what he could after the fact, and Rosie did not mind that. Sometimes, she preferred it.

When it came to marriage, Ray had done a very good job. Rosie had never considered them to have marriage problems. Yes, they had arguments from time to time, but they were silly things that the two of them would laugh about later. Ray's issue was he was so good at juggling problems that he sometimes forgot his wife's interest in them or how he felt about them.

When Ray came into the house after his pastoral office hours that Sunday evening and saw his wife watching him over her book, he bent down to kiss her, not worried about her losing her place.

"Evening, lovely." He murmured as he straightened, then walked over to his chair.

"And lovely evening." Rosie finished their ritual.

She waited until her husband was comfortable before closing her book with a snap and setting it aside with a soft thud.

"Yes, dear?" Ray asked. Rosie had never said he was not a smart man.

Rosie crossed her arms and fixed her husband with her fiercest glare before saying, "Well, what do you think of Harkin?"

Instead of cowering from her gaze, Ray only frowned, "I think you don't have a very high opinion of the young man." Ray pretended not to notice his wife's nostrils flare but added, "He seems a decent enough fellow, and he is definitely a little sweet on our Emilia. You should have seen the way he was looking at her before church." He finished with a chuckle.

"Oh, I have seen. Always hanging around the café. He is not sweet; he is a stalker."

This time Ray turned his frown on his wife, "Now dear, just because you are a little overprotective, it's no excuse to go running down a man's character."

Rosie, very maturely and very articulately, stuck her tongue out at her husband, who only winked in response. When Rosie could keep the smile from her lips, for she would not be distracted, she picked up the conversation where they left off.

"Fine! Maybe not a stalker, or at least one I could convict, but I don't think he is good for her."

Ray, who had removed one shoe and was beginning to polish it, stopped to look at his wife, "Because of something he has done or because of her past?"

"Don't turn this around to me. The program and counseling all caution against it, and you know it."

"They do," He admitted, "and the young Mr. Harkin knows and respects that." Ray smiled at the surprised look on his wife's face, "Here I thought you had probably been eavesdropping. Emilia told him some details about her past and that they could only be friends right now, and he accepted that."

If Ray had gotten any better over the years reading his wife's facial expressions, he would have called it a look of grudging approval that passed over her features.

"He has?" She asked.

"Yes, although, I dare say I think Emilia could be ready for a relationship in this stage of her recovery."

"She most certainly is not!" Rosie interjected.

"Do you know something I don't?" Ray asked.

This time, Rosie only winked as she picked her book back up.

***

Harkin sat at home, and for the first time, he looked around his apartment. To his dismay, he began to wonder if anyone really lived there. From where his chair sat, he could see into the kitchen. The heavy wooden table and set of chairs that had come with the apartment and which he did now wonder if they were all hand-carved, thinking back he was sure the realtor had said something about that. Every surface gleamed immaculately, even the cabinet doors that he rubbed with old English every week to make sure they shone. If he could see through the wooden doors, he would see the spotless two plates, two bowls, two sets of silverware, and he would see one simple set of cooking pans.

Yes, it is clean, Harkin thought, but it's somehow sparse for a room that has been used every day for five years. Then there was the front room, where his chair sat.

"Only my chair." Harkin said aloud just to disturb the sudden silence he felt.

He realized that his chair was the only piece of personality in the house. It was a heavy, wooden handcrafted piece. It was stained a dark cherry with a few spots that were fading, although Harkin treated it often, the burgundy cushion that he had found for it made a wonderful contrast to the wood, and it was, Harkin sadly realized, his prize possession.

Sitting next to Harkin's chair was a small end table where his laptop sat when he was not using it, and perched behind both was a floor lamp. It was a basic thing, just something so that he would not have to get up to get the light when it got dark. Looking up, Harkin smiled a little. He could see through the frosted shade that there was not even a bulb in the ceiling fixture. Not that it mattered, he continued to think to himself, there is nothing for it to shed any light on. There were no other chairs, sofas, or couches in the front room. He did not own a television and therefore had no need for an entertainment center.

"How have you been living like this?" He asked the empty room and tried to close his mind before it could answer.

Harkin failed in closing out the answer as he heard Benji's voice telling him that he could have lived his life. Harkin realized he had not heard all of Benji's meaning. He had called Harkin an emptiness making a mockery of life, and Harkin had not even challenged that declaration. Perhaps, because he was not wrong, Harkin thought to himself, afraid to even voice the words. Maybe it was time for him to listen to the ones who were pointing out his addiction. He sighed at the empty room.

Harkin looked at the church bulletin sitting next to his laptop, where Emily had written her phone number. He picked up his phone and began to type, pausing only before hitting the send button. He let his thumb find the backspace icon then he held it down. He dialed the number, this time committing to the send button. When she answered in the middle of the first ring, Harkin nearly dropped his phone.

"It took you long enough." Emily said in the way of greeting.

"How did you know it was me?" Harkin asked, still trying to stifle his surprise.

"It's nearly midnight. Who else is going to call this late other than the guy who has been putting it off all day?" She asked, and he could hear her smile.

"About that, running off and just leaving behind a phone number doesn't exactly send a guy a clear signal." Harkin explained, and he knew she could tell that he was smiling, too.

"Sorry," Emily said tentatively, "it was something Ray said."

"Want to talk about it?" Harkin responded just as tentatively.

"What are we going to be to each other? I know that is crazy to ask you when literary you could just want to be a friendly, recognized regular at a coffee shop, and we really only just met, but I don't think that is what you want."

"I think we have created a catchphrase for this. We are just those kinds of friends."

"Cute," she said with a half-hearted giggle, "but I'm serious, and you did not answer the question. What are we going to be to each other?"

"Not that I'm trying to avoid your question again," Harkin started to answer.

"Sure, sure." Emily interrupted, chiding him teasingly.

"But," He continued, dragging out the word, "I don't know how to answer your question. You went from something that you heard this morning to asking about us. You might be making a parallel, but I'm chasing tangents."

"Yeah, like a high school freshman who is failing geometry." She pointed out with another snicker, "What I am asking is,"

She trailed off, and Harkin waited long enough that he was beginning to wonder if she was going to hand upon him before he prompted, "What you are asking is?"

"What I am asking is are we the stars that lead each other into the storm or the island that we wash up upon after our lives were wrecked?"

"Stars or islands? Those are the only two options?" Harkin asked.

"I guess there is also the storm, but I don't think either one of us wants to be that for the other. So, what will it be?" she asked.

"I would like to think you've already been through your storm, and now I'm here." Harkin chuckled, "I don't know if that's a good thing or not, and I'm definitely sure if that's any comfort, but I don't want to believe that I'm leading you into the storm."

"And I want to believe that I won't do the same to you. For all the comfort that is worth." Emily admitted, "But, we can't know that."

"Isn't this where your type of people like to say to have faith?"

"Did you get all that from one sermon?" Emily asked sarcastically.

"I'm not pushing you." Harkin said, ignoring her snide remark.

"I know." She relented.

"But?" He continued to prompt her.

"What if you didn't *have* to push? What if I wanted to do this? Could we?" Emily spat out the questions seriously and quickly.

"And what about your recovery?" Harkin noticed the note of concern in his voice and was sure Emily had as well.

"The advice is to wait a year. It's about giving myself a window of time for self-discovery without romantic entanglements and creating a new kind of dependency that could prove to be just as unhealthy as the first. Also, it is to help eliminate distractions from the whole process."

"And how long has it been for you?" Harkin pressed.

"Ten months." Emily answered honestly.

"That's not a year." He observed, and she could hear the humor in his voice.

"No, it isn't," She agreed with a small giggle, "but I've had time to discover who I am, and I don't think you would let me turn you into a distraction from my recovery."

"Okay. How do we do this?"

"I think you ask me to dinner." Emily said, and now he could hear her smiling.

"How about breakfast?"

"I think that could work." Emily agreed.

"This morning?" Harkin asked.

"Umm, sounds like you might be pushing."

"No, I'm not. If I was pushing, I would ask about right now."

"Now?" She asked with another incredulous giggle.

"It's after midnight, so technically it's morning. Why not?"

This time, Emily did not restrain her laughter as she blurted out, "You're nervous!"

"Why do you say that?" Harkin asked, feigning innocent curiosity.

"Because there is a certain degree of insufferable hopelessness happening in this conversation, and it's not my fault."

"As to whose fault it is, we may have to agree to disagree, but what about it? Breakfast, right now?"

"Sure."

***

Under all of his newfound realizations, Harkin could hardly claim to be a gentleman. Still, he did not like the idea of Emily walking the six blocks to his place, but she had insisted. However, when he opened the door to see her standing on his front step, he could hardly complain. After knocking, she had turned away from the door to watch the street.

Harkin had unknowingly grown so accustomed to the coffee shop attire that he was surprised to feel his breath leave him at the simple sight of her. The way the early morning darkness caressed and shaded her red hair so that it showed a deep crimson as it cascaded down her back onto an oversized green sweatshirt that hid her curves yet still attracted the eye with an unmatched allure to travel her form all the way down to the black leggings she was wearing that enticed him to study every delicate contour from the exquisite sweep of her hips to the intricate lines of her ankles. Emily, Harkin realized too late, had a figure that his eyes wanted to explore, and he realized that his eyes were doing just that only when he felt the intensity of the blue, sapphire jewels of her eyes burning into him.

In that singular moment, Harkin understood what she had meant when Emily had said she had accidentally kissed him. It became clear as he felt his fingers tracing the arch of her back as his hand came to rest just under the hem of her sweatshirt against her smooth skin. That surge of electricity from the feel of her skin against his, sparking in him a spreading warmth of passion he had never experienced until his lips met hers. The seductive curve of her thin lips that had until this moment been an unknown temptation held him enchanted in a sensual yearning that only broke when he felt her teeth drag across his bottom lip as she pulled away only far enough that he still felt her breath tease through his parted lips and across his tongue, letting him savor the sweetness of her exhalation.

"So, this kind of thing does happen around you." Harkin said softly as he lost himself in her eyes.

"Do you mean that was an accident?" And he could hear a real note of concern in her voice.

"Oh, I wanted to do it, but I didn't mean to."

Her lips that he was still intently watching curved into a provocative smirk, "Don't worry, I won't let you do it again. Accidently." He felt himself leaning in when one soft finger pressed against his lips, "Ah, now I thought I was coming over here for breakfast?"

"Of course, come in." He said against her finger, noticing the way she bit her bottom lip as she watched his lips move against her finger.

With a noticeably great effort, he let his hand slide away from the small of her back as he stepped out of her way then gestured for her to come inside. He pulled out her chair, not to be polite or chivalrous but so that he could relish the touch of her as she brushed against him.

"So, what are we having?" She asked, trying not to react to the casual way his fingers trailed across her shoulder as he moved away from her chair.

He grabbed two plates from the counter and sat one in front of her with an apologetic look, "Perhaps, I should have warned you, my cooking skills are basic at best."

Emily looked down at the plate to see blueberry pancakes with a dollop of whipped cream and two strawberries as a garnish.

Darren Finney

"Just happen to have the makings for a romantic breakfast lying around?" Emily asked as she dipped one of the strawberries in the whipped cream and slowly brought it to her lips.

Harkin was so enthralled waiting for her to take a bite that he did not realize that he had not answered.

"Harkin?"

"Yeah. No." He answered.

Emily watched him give his head that nearly imperceptible shake as if warding off a bad memory, or the makings of a good memory, Emily thought with a small flip deep in her stomach.

"I may have bought it after church." Harkin admitted.

She laughed at the sheepish look on his face before taking a bite of the strawberry. Obviously savoring the taste while she chewed, Harkin was further captivated, watching the way the muscles in her jaw flexed with the motion as his eyes followed the delicate lines of her jaw back to the small bead of red juice still clinging to her lips. As the tip of her tongue flicked out to slowly trace her lips, he picked up his fork and did a very pointed job of trying to focus on his plate so that he missed the tantalizing wink she had given him.

"So, breakfast was always the plan, but I can only hope that four in the morning wasn't." She attested after swallowing.

He smiled as he chewed, then clearing his mouth, he said, "No, four in the morning was not part of the plan."

"But what you said this morning about having to be just friends?" Emily implored.

"What about what you said tonight?" Harkin replied.

"No, you bought this stuff before that." She pointed out.

"Maybe we could be those kinds of friends." Harkin answered, giving her a shrug and a ghost of his charming smile.

"Would that be enough for you?" Emily asked, and Harkin felt her eyes boring into him.

Harkin sighed, then sat down his fork before saying, "Honestly, no. But I said I wasn't going to push you, so if that is all you can have right now, then it will have to be enough."

Harkin starred imploringly into her eyes, trying to figure out her reaction, but he could perceive nothing. He could not tell if she was upset or angry, happy or ecstatic. She sat there quietly torturing him as she reached down to pick up the other strawberry from her plate without responding, then wordlessly stemmed it with her fingernails. She slowly walked around the table, trailing the fingers of her empty hand along its edge and enjoying the ways his eyes seemed to travel her body with each step until she stood over him, still sitting in his chair. She casually slid his plate out of her way as she sat down on the table and brought one leg over to straddle his chair. A faint smile pulled at the corners of her mouth as he unconsciously slid his hands up her calves and let them rest on her thighs just above her knees.

"And if it's not enough?" She asked in an enticing voice as she ran the strawberry across her lips.

Harkin stood, toppling his chair with the backs of his knees as he let his hands continue to glide up the gentle sweep of her hips to rest on the bare skin of her waist underneath the sweater before firmly pulling her into him. She held the strawberry to his lips with a wink. As he parted his lips, intending to take a bite, she pulled it away, placing it in her teeth and wrapping her arms around his neck. He leaned in to take a slow bite of the strawberry in her mouth, feeling the pressure of her teeth again as she sank her teeth into his bottom lip and moaned into his mouth as she savored the taste of the fruit before releasing his lip from her bite.

Emily laid her head onto his shoulder then nuzzled into his neck. As her legs tightened around him, she felt his hands slide to her back to encircle her.

"Can you just hold me like this for a little while?" She asked, her warm breath teasing the skin of his neck. When she felt his thumb begin to stroke her back, she said, "Thank you."

Harkin could not have guessed how much time had passed while he stood in his kitchen silently holding Emily in his arms, but when he next saw her eyes as she lifted her head, the sunrise was reflected in them.

"Good morning." She said with a nervous smile.

"Good morning. Not that I'm complaining but did I just hold you while you slept?" He asked.

"I didn't sleep, but I would be lying if I said I didn't feel refreshed." Emily looked down guiltily, "I didn't mean to make you stand all this time."

Harkin slid his hands back down to her thighs that were still pressed against his hips. As he watched her bite her lip as his grip tightened, he asked, "Did you hear me complain?"

"No," She said, her tone slipping into a mock annoyance, "I guess I should apologize for letting breakfast get cold too."

"It's still early. We can try again later if you like."

"I'd like that." Emily said with a sincere smile that stopped Harkin's heart faster than her kiss had.

In the second before his heart started beating again, Harkin used a knuckle to lift her chin and bring her lips to his. When he pulled away, she smiled again.

"That had better not be another accident." She said.

"No. I fully intended that one."

"Good." He felt her eyes exploring his thoughts as she stroked his cheek then asked, "Am I real to you? More than a friend? Because that is not all I want to be."

For the first time, Emily felt his brown eyes pour into her as he asked, "And what do you want to be?"

"More." She answered with force behind the one word that rocked him.

"I would like that."

"Would you really?" She asked seriously as she leaned back to better examine him.

"Yes." He replied, slight bewilderment showing in his features.

"That would mean being honest with me."

"I have never lied to you."

Her smile revealed her sad understanding, "We are both recovering addicts in our own right, and we have to learn that truth is not exclusive to deceit. It requires openness too."

Harkin sighed, dropping his head on her shoulder before saying, "I think I know where this is going. There really is no winning against a pretty girl."

"Told you." She said with a laugh, "But I mean it. I want to know how your addiction started. What happened between you and your parents."

"I believe I asked you first."

"No, you said you had questions, but I asked first." She clarified.

"I think this will be a conversation I need to sit down for."

Emily shrugged, then pushed herself off the table, letting her body glide against his until her feet reached the floor. She winked, wrapping her fingers in his, then pulled him into his front room.

"You don't have a couch." She said, looking around the room.

"Hasn't really been a problem until now." Harkin said in the way of an explanation.

Again, Emily shrugged before pushing him into his chair and sitting across his lap.

She flipped her hair back over her shoulder and smiled, "Now, no more distractions. Talk to me."

Harkin gave her a shrug of his own before smiling, "I really don't know what you want me to say."

"Alright," She said, a sternness hardening her blue eyes, "let's start with an easy one. Does your family share your addiction?"

"How would I know?" Harkin asked, the coldness seeping into the edges of his eyes.

"Do you not talk to them? At all?" Emily asked, astonishment in her voice.

"No."

"When was the last time?"

"When I left." Harkin answered.

"That has to change." She declared.

✳✳✳

To My Unkindled Love,

I would not lie to you, child. It is a frightening thing to prepare yourself for that kind of relationship with God. As with any real relationship, it is fraught with anxieties and doubts, triumphs and defeats, worry and love, but next comes the true fear of humbly asking Him to remove your shortcomings. Not just the shortcomings you want to overcome either, but all of them. Even the ones that you do not consider failings, and the ones you keep hidden even from yourself. I know that it scares you, and that's okay because it should. Because it needs to in order for it to do you any good. If you were not afraid to confess your deepest and darkest, then my child, you have neither gone deep enough nor shone a light far enough into that depth to see that your soul goes darker. If you were not afraid to confess, then you, my dear sweet one, probably weren't confessing anything meaningful. Fear comes before confession, and faith comes after. Forgiveness? Well, that'll come.

Maybe that is why the verse starts the way it does. Have you ever noticed that, dear one? Not when but if, and not even just if. It starts with but if a double uncertainty. A fear, perhaps? Or maybe anxiety? Either way, it is definitely a challenge. Read it for yourself. "But if we confess our sins to Him, He is faithful and just to forgive us our sins and to cleanse us from all wickedness." (1 John 1:9 NLT)

Don't let the thought of your wickedness frighten you from being clean of it. As you ask God to remove your character flaws and shortcomings, you also take actions that give God greater ability to work changes in your life. That is, after all, the reason to make the decision to accept the slow fight of surrender in your life. Change.

I know the truth of it too, sweet darling. Change is perhaps the thing that frightens you most. It is perhaps the thing that challenges and terrifies you the most. What if you cannot change? Would if you cannot sustain change? What if the change leaves you worse than you are? Well, dear child, what if it doesn't? What if you did not have to do it alone?

Evermore,

Your Kindred Heart

Chapter Eight

To whom it may concern,

Of course, I can be your friend. Only as long as you are my enemy. Only then can I trust and know you. When you become my friend, then I can no longer trust your intentions. When you become a friend, you would think your intentions pure and good only for them to become so much more dangerous to something already so very tenuous.

Why then can I be your friend? Because you should not trust me. I will always have good intentions, and it will always be dangerous. How dangerous? Only you would know. After all, I remember the way it felt more than anything else. That moment of desire and regret. Of joy and pain. Do I wish that on anybody else? Absolutely! You will never be freer than when you accept that you want to be shackled to something. Mind you, I'm not the one who said it needed to be some artificial thing. You can cling to your substances and your fillers, but I can promise you that is only empty weight. A long rope and a short tree. A gun without a trigger. A heart without love.

No, you need the feeling. The warmth of their lips on yours. Their heartbeat reverberating in your chest as you pull them ever closer—the tremble of their fingers as they entwine with yours. No, dear, you need to be a captive. You want the prison. Otherwise, you cannot cope.

How do I know? Your guess is as good as mine. I don't have a clue. I offer you the prison from the grave. My rope was not too long, and my gun had a trigger. The burdensome weight was crushing. Perhaps that is not quite right. Perhaps it is not a grave, just rehab. Just another junkie needing a fix. Another boozer searching for another bottle. That's who you're asking for advice— another recovering addict who lived just a little too much life. Chase your feelings if you want. Have your high. Just remember, neither of us wins when I say, "I told you so!".

Evermore,

Your Betrayed Deception

***

At least she looked beautiful, Harkin told himself. Emily was wearing a light blue and pink floral printed flared skater skirt with a ruffle-trimmed neckline and shoulders that had a covered button placket that draws attention to a darted bodice and fitted waist. Not that Harkin knew any of that, he just knew how she looked in it. He stood at the front bumper, watching her walk around the car to take his hand in the driveway. The skirt masked the gentle sweep and sway of her hips as she walked that his eyes would have followed to the smooth contours of her firm thighs, but it revealed what the green sweatshirt had hidden, and now he felt his eyes traveling up the elegant curves from her waistline over her torso. His eyes drinking her in until they met hers as they flashed that dangerous hue that told him she knew he was doing it again. At least something good would come from today, he continued to think.

Harkin was still not sure how breakfast had turned into this. He felt like he was being guided through his own twelve-step program, and the problem was he still did not know how he felt about that. Emily slid her fingers down his arm and entwined her fingers in his with a small smile. He was beginning to think he would do anything for that smile, even this.

"Are you ready?" Emily asked, and Harkin realized he had been silently exploring those sapphire depths again.

"Does it matter?" He answered nonchalantly.

"Of course, it does!" She exclaimed, "If you're really not ready to do this, it won't be good for you."

"You'll stay with me?" Harkin asked, maybe pleaded.

"I'm here, aren't I?" Emily responded, giving his hand a gentle squeeze.

He raised the back of her hand to his lips then kissed it softly. As he lowered their hands to his side, he saw that smile dancing in her eyes now. She kept that same light in her eyes as she nearly had to drag him to the front steps. She stopped in front of the door and held him in that same compassionate gaze.

"Are you sure?" She asked.

"Yes." He answered, careful to keep that nonchalant tone out of his voice this time.

She held her hand up to knock on the door, pausing only to give him one last look before rapping her knuckles against the hardwood. The woman who opened the door was not who Harkin remembered. She was not who he had expected either. The woman was a nurse, blonde and young. She was not the woman Harkin thought lived here.

"I'm sorry, ma'am, I think we have the wrong house." Harkin apologized.

The woman tilted her head, eyeing Harkin curiously before saying, "You look older than the picture, but I think I recognize you. Harkin, you are the Lindsey's son?"

"Yes." Harkin said, surprised.

"Please, come in. I'm sure she'll be glad you came." The nurse said, beckoning them in as she stepped aside.

She left them standing in the front hall while she stepped into the back of the house. Harkin looked over to Emily, who had a concerned look on her face.

"So, you don't know why a nurse is here?" She asked.

"I told you, I haven't talked to them since I left. But they're older. Maybe they needed a little help."

"Maybe." Emily agreed, biting her lip.

The nurse came back into the hall, followed by the woman Harkin had been expecting.

"Hi, mom." Harkin plaintively offered.

Beatrice Lindsey froze at the sight of her son. In that moment, Harkin still did not recognize his mother. Her once free-flowing auburn hair had gone mostly gray and was pulled into a tight bun that was fraying from neglect. Her clothes were well-worn and stained from several days of wear. He remembered the well-manicured, well-dressed powerful woman that ran his childhood. He did not know this woman that looked helpless and lost.

"Harkin?" She asked.

"It's me, mom. What's going on?" Harkin asked, gesturing to the nurse.

"Oh, dear," She said, tears filling her eyes, "I wanted you to come back, but not like this." Beatrice looked at Emily, "Who is this?"

"This is Emily. Emily meet Beatrice Lindsey, my mother."

"Bea, dear." Beatrice said as she gave Emily an affectionate hug.

"It is so nice to meet you." Emily offered warmly.

"Thank you, dear. I wish I was a little better put together, but a woman mustn't complain."

"I don't know about that." Emily said with a small laugh.

Bea smiled at her, then said, "Now let's take a look at this young man you brought back to me."

Harkin felt the eyes of both women turn to him, and he fought the urge to sigh.

"You look healthy and well, honey." Bea told her son.

"I am."

"It will mean a lot to him that you came." Bea added forlornly.

"Mom, what's going on?" Harkin repeated.

"Follow me, honey." Bea said as she turned in the doorway.

He felt Emily's hand slide into his as he was made to follow his mother. He tried to smile for her, but he felt the tension building in him, and he was not sure if Emily understood he was trying to be comforting.

Harkin remembered the long walk down this hall. When Nora was here, he would feel the dread build in him when he would come home from school, and he was not sure how he would find her. Eventually, he had to stop leaving her side because it was too hard to walk the hall to see her. He was too afraid of what he would find one day.

Walking this old familiar hall again, Harkin felt that same dreadful fear rising in him, and he did not know if it had to do with the memories of his sister or the way his mother was acting. Part of him was confused. Harkin had not seen nor spoken to his father in eighteen years, and to feel this way about how he might find his father surprised him. Harkin did not hate his father, but he would not have thought that he loved him either. Eugene Lindsey was never who Harkin thought of when he thought of a good man. To be fair, he did not think of himself either.

His mother stepped inside the room she had always called the parlor, and Harkin froze at the threshold. For him, this would always be the room Nora died in. Now, it was as if very little had changed. There was still a hospice bed against the wall next to the large picture window, but lying in bed was Eugene. Much like with his mother, Harkin did not recognize the man his father had become. Eugene Lindsey had always seemed like a force to be reckoned with until Nora had gotten sick, and even then, he may have been broken, but Harkin would not have called him weak. Looking at his father now, Harkin could only think that he looked frail. Eugene's eyes were closed, and Harkin could not tell if he was sleeping, but he did not seem to notice as Bea entered the room and sat in a chair beside his bed.

When Harkin made to step into the room, he felt the tug on his arm. He turned to see Emily pale and rigid.

"I'm sorry. I can't." She said shakily.

Harkin gave her a small, sad smile, "It's okay, I understand." He fished in his pocket for his keys, "Here, take my car back, I will get a ride. Call you later?"

She took his keys, nodding her head, all the while never taking her eyes off of Eugene.

"Are you going to be okay?" Harkin asked.

Again, she only nodded.

Harkin stepped closer then kissed her brow before asking, "Are you sure?"

"I need to go." She answered.

"Call me later." He said as she turned to leave.

"Your friend not staying?" His mother asked as Harkin moved deeper into the room.

"No. How bad is it?" Harkin responded.

"They are just trying to keep him comfortable right now." Bea answered in a voice that told Harkin she had run out of tears to cry.

"What is it?"

"Liver failure, and now his kidneys are shutting down. He never stopped drinking long enough for them to consider placing him on the transplant list, and now it wouldn't do any good."

How long does he have?" Harkin asked somberly.

"Days, maybe. Sometimes, he wakes up and seems to know what is going on. I'm sorry."

Harkin shrugged, "It's not like you could have gotten a hold of me to tell me."

"I thought about trying before he got this bad, but I wasn't sure what I would've said." His mother told him, not with any cruelty in her voice, but as if she were trying to defend herself.

"How bad was the drinking?"

An uneasy silence settled over the room until Harkin finally stopped looking at his father and turned to face his mother. She had been silently crying, he realized. She had not made a sound, not one wretched sob, as the tears streaked her cheeks. Harkin walked over and awkwardly hugged his mother, who started crying harder into his shoulder. Harkin was not sure how long they stayed like that, but it did seem quite sometime later before his mother's sobs subsided. When she regained herself, she stood up and held her son at arm's length, examining him like she had only then realized who he was.

"Are you hungry?" She asked, "Neighbors have been sending all kinds of food. I couldn't possibly eat it all myself. I could warm us up something. Will you stay for dinner?"

He could see the frantic plea in her eyes as he said, "Sure, mom, I'll stay."

Harkin thought she was going to cry again, but she smiled and hugged him before rushing into the kitchen.

"Do you need help with anything?" He called after her.

"No, just keep an eye on your father for me." She called back.

Harkin sat down in the chair his mother had been using and looked at his father. Harkin nearly jumped when he realized his father was watching him. Eugene had turned his head with his eyes focused on Harkin, and there was a tear still clinging to the corner of his eye.

"Hey, dad." Harkin said softly.

When Eugene made to move one feeble hand, Harkin reached out to take it in his. Eugene tried to squeeze Harkin's hand back, but there was not any strength left there, and he closed his eyes. Harkin sat there holding onto his father's feeble and withered hand, waiting for him to open his eyes again. His mother came in carrying two plates before his father opened his eyes. Harkin realized that there were silent tears on his own cheeks this time, and he stood, letting his mother take her chair as he brushed them away. He took a plate from her before sitting on the couch that still sat against the opposite wall from the bed.

"Not that I don't love seeing you, but what brought you back?" Bea asked her son, "It wasn't Emily, was it?"

"In a manner of speaking." Harkin started to explain.

"Are you getting married? Is she pregnant?" His mother interrupted.

"No. No, nothing like that. She has been helping me to realize that maybe I have been wrong."

"Wrong?"

"I've been so angry with you and dad for so long that I have just built my entire life around it. Apparently, that's not healthy."

Bea looked at her husband before fixing her gaze back on her son, "Seems it's been healthier than some of the alternatives. So, this Emily. What? Is she your therapist?"

"No. Just somebody that has seen some of the unhealthy ways to deal."

Bea nodded, "Why are you still angry?"

"Still?" There was a flash of the darker side of her son behind his eyes when he asked.

Bea did not back down, "I know you will never forgive us. I've accepted that, but yes, why are you still angry with us? Why haven't you just forgotten us?"

"Because I still love you." Harkin said bitterly, "And I cannot stop no matter how much I want to."

If her son's revelation shocked her, Bea did not show it, but her voice remained calm as she said, "And no matter how much you wanted to be able to hate us, we never stopped loving you."

Harkin did not answer but focused on his plate, and the two of them finished their meal in silence. When Harkin stood to take their plates into the kitchen, there was a knock at the door.

"I'll get it. It is probably the pastor. He usually comes by of an evening." Bea told her son.

Harkin did not give it much thought while he washed the dishes until he returned to find Benjamin standing next to his father's bed. Benjamin looked drastically different, having traded in the faded overalls for a clean shirt and dress pants. Gone was the shovel, but he held a Bible firmly grasped in his hands. There was a flicker of surprise flash across Benjamin's features at the sight of Harkin, but he recovered well with a warm smile.

"Harkin, this is Pastor Ben." Bea said in the way of introduction.

Harkin shook hands pleasantly as he answered his mother, "We've met."

"Oh?" Bea said with a modicum of confusion.

"Yes, we have talked when he has come to pay respects to Miss Nora." Benjamin explained.

Bea turned to eye each man suspiciously as if she thought they were hiding something, and her suspicions were made clear as she fixed Benjamin with a gaze that Harkin had learned to fear growing up before saying, "You never mentioned that."

To his credit, Harkin thought, Benjamin did not seem to back down from that look as he replied, "Mr. Lindsey and I had spoken on the matter a time or two, ma'am. It was his request that I not bring it up to you."

"Oh." Bea repeated, this time her eyes wandering over to where her husband lay.

Harkin's eyes followed hers, then came back to Benji, and he wondered if he had just heard a pastor lie or, more surprising, if he had just heard Benji lie. Harkin could not bring himself to contemplate whether the conversation was real or if his father had really felt that way.

"Bea, dear, I will come by tomorrow. You have company tonight." Benjamin said, and Bea nodded her acceptance.

"I'll see you out." The nurse said, surprising Harkin, who had forgotten she was there.

He watched as they walked out of the room together, and Harkin felt a moment of déjà vu that he could not place.

"Since when did you let a pastor in here?" Harkin asked, genuinely curious.

"Seems you are just as friendly with him." His mother answered defensively.

Harkin frowned sympathetically, "I didn't mean it like that. We just never were a church family, I didn't think."

"We weren't." His mother agreed, "I started going after you left. Your father took some convincing, but he did come with me. I'm afraid when he gets to Heaven's gate, he may still smell a little like smoke, maybe a few singed hairs." His mother said with an affectionate smile that Harkin did not fully understand, but before he could say anything, she continued, "It was a decision I made in my heart to go to church, but I think your father only made the decision with his head. Don't get me wrong, he tried, but I think that is why he could still be found in the bar most nights. It was easier for me, I think, to let go of a lot of the fear, but he just couldn't find the same peace."

"That's nice, mom." Harkin ineffectually offered.

Bea smiled at her son's attempt to understand, but she knew he still struggled with it, "I pray for you, you know?"

"Why do you do that?" He asked.

"Because I'm your mother. I worry about you, and I love you. Because I worry that I made a mistake not taking you to church growing up, but I can see now God has a way of working it out. Some of those Sunday school stories that everyone just seems to know talk about that, and I don't always get it, but I'm starting to understand it." She hugged her son again, "I'm glad you're here."

※※

To My Unkindled Love,

Understand, one of the greatest actions you can take toward change is making sure others know your intent to change. This is where you have to assess all of the ways you could have possibly caused harm to others and also yourself. You then must make yourself ready and willing to restore these relationships through both words and actions.

Society calls it the golden rule. "Do to others as you would like them to do to you." (Luke 6:31 NLT) Unfortunately, we have to be realistic because you have already taken it one step further. You have to do more than change. You have to repair! You have to make a list of all the people you have harmed and become willing to make amends to them all. You have to have remorse in order to have forgiveness. You have to understand your rights and your wrongs. You also must make it clear to those around you that you have reached such an understanding. There is, after all, a reason the term is amending change.

Evermore,

Your Kindred Heart

Chapter Nine

To Whom It May Concern;

If it were easy, everyone would do it. That's funny, isn't it? In that bitter sort of way, I suppose, because there is no part of that statement that is true. People are lazy. They wouldn't do the simplest things, much less should you rely on them to do the easiest things. People only do those when they have to. Never mind the things that are hard. People just don't do that.

Think I'm lying? Look at yourself. Do you really expect me to believe you would be doing this if someone wasn't making you? Do you really expect me to believe that you would keep doing it if they weren't there to keep making you? No, people need to be *forced or led. Some special cases need to be both. People don't take the initiative to do the hard stuff, and they certainly don't brag about it when they know they didn't do it for any selfless reason.*

What does that mean? Selfless? Yeah, I imagine that is a hard concept for you. It isn't for everybody. Now that strikes closer to true than most of us would care to admit. If it were easy, everyone would do it, but not everyone can be selfless. Not everyone can deny themselves to do something greater than themselves. Not everyone can forget what they want or forget what they had enough to lay it all aside in a pursuit that isn't all about what they want. Not that anyone expects you to anymore, either.

Evermore,

Your Selfless Greed

✳✳✳

Despite his mother's protests, Harkin slept on the old sofa in the parlor instead of his old bedroom. He felt a small twinge of guilt when he woke up to find that his mother had covered him up with the old quilt from his bed while he slept. He sat up, rubbing the sleep from his face and looking around. Across the room, next to where his father lay, stood the nurse already tending to the machines and checking his vitals. Harkin was aware that she had left sometime during the night, but he could not remember exactly when, and he did not wake when she had returned. It was a crude thought he knew, but he wondered how much she was charging for this kind of full-service treatment. She interrupted his detestable thoughts when she noticed he was awake and offered a heartening smile instead of a greeting.

"Your mother isn't up yet, but the coffee is ready in the kitchen if you need a cup." She informed him as she returned to the task at hand.

"Thank you, ma'am." Harkin said, getting to his feet.

"Klarissa."

"Harkin."

"I know."

"Right." Harkin said, shaking his head walking out of the room.

When he returned to the room holding a cup of coffee, Klarissa had turned to face him with her hands clasped in front of her, holding something that Harkin could not quite tell what it was. Seeing his eyes travel to it, she held it out to him.

"He asked that I didn't give it to you in front of your mother, but he wanted you to have this. He was beginning to lose motor skills in his hands by that point, so I wrote it for him, but he told me what to write. He wasn't sure if you would come at all, but he wanted it to be here just in case. I don't think he would mind if I go ahead and give it to you now, but I still don't think he would like for you to have it out in front of your mother."

Harkin took it from her and stuck it into the pocket of his suit jacket that was still lying on the back of the sofa, "Thank you. Were things getting bad between them?"

The nurse gave him a confused look, "I'm sorry, I don't know what you mean."

"Between my parents. It seems like there were a lot of things that he did not want her to know."

Klarissa sighed, Harkin could not tell for sure, but he was almost certain that it had been an impatient sigh. He was about to object to her very reaction even though he could not for the life of him figure out why he should be testing her patience; however, she spoke before he had the chance.

"No, things were not bad." She answered, and Harkin almost thought he heard a twinge of anger now, "In fact, he cares for her very much, and I think he just didn't want to use you to break her heart."

Harkin felt the insult she had directed at him, and he felt his jaw clench as he held back a retort. By the smug expression of disapproving satisfaction on her face, Harkin could tell she had noticed his reaction too. Perhaps, that was why she tried to soften the edge to her words, Harkin thought as she continued to speak to him.

"I know it isn't my place, but he did seem to really care about you, too."

Harkin shook off her assurances, "So, do you do this kind of thing often? Make the coffee and offer the family counseling, or are they paying extra for that?" He said, and he could tell that they both knew he was still bitter about her comments.

"Sometimes people's family won't do it for them, so I don't have a choice. Some families don't forgive each other until they're gone. Why do you hate him?" She fired back, there was no malice in her words, but there did not need to be either. Harkin felt them just the same.

Harkin sat back down on the sofa and took another slow sip of the coffee, giving Klarissa the universal eyebrow arch and tip of the cup to say it was good. He sat quietly, remembering that night so long ago. He had taken to sleeping on the same sofa that he now sat on so that he could be by his sister's side all the time. He knew her time was coming soon; she had stopped waking up, and even before that, it had stopped being a coherent consciousness. The last time that she had been properly alert, she had pulled him to her bedside to sing happy birthday to him, and to this day, Harkin still held a bittersweet feeling toward his birthday as he remembered his baby sister singing to him. What he remembered most was that last night, his father had come into the parlor and stood next to Nora's bed. If Eugene had known that Harkin was awake, he did not acknowledge it as he stood there silently sobbing over his daughter. Harkin had laid there at sixteen watching his father cry, too afraid to do anything. After several minutes, Eugene had bent down over his daughter's bed, kissing her brow and running his fingers over her brittle hair. Straightening up, he reached over to the machines next to the bed, and the quiet hums and rhythmic pumping noises that had become a constant in the house stopped. In the new silence, Harkin could hear his father's sobs now.

'What did you do?' Harkin remembered asking, and in response, his father had jumped in surprise and left the room without saying anything.

Harkin met Klarissa's eyes, "He gave up on her."

"You have to know that's not true." She said in disbelief, and although she said it like a statement, Harkin could hear the question.

"He came in here and shut off the systems that were keeping her alive." Harkin answered.

"I wasn't there, but I have been in that situation enough to know that at a point, all those machines don't keep someone alive. Most of the time, they just keep them in pain. He didn't give up on her. He gave her a chance to stop hurting. You're just too selfish to let go of the pain, and right now might be your last chance." Harkin was quiet, and Klarissa sighed, "Never mind. Listen, I'm going to leave for a couple of hours to make a few other visits. Normally, Bea is up by now, but I imagine her schedule and routine are a little out of sorts right now, so you will need to sit with him until she gets around. Can you do that?"

"Sure." Harkin said with a shrug.

"Let me rephrase. Will you do that?"

"Yes." Harkin answered, this time an edge sharpening his voice.

"Good." Klarissa replied, her voice holding a bite of its own as she walked out of the room.

Harkin waited until he heard the front close behind her before he moved from the sofa to the chair next to his father's bed. For the first time that morning, Harkin let his eyes settle on his father's face, and looking back at him were Eugene's yellowed eyes. Harkin felt a wave of self-loathing wash over him as he wondered if his father had been listening to his conversation with the nurse. That initial wave was followed by a powerful current of indignation at the thought of worrying about what his father would think, of anger at himself for feeling this way and anger at his father for putting him in this position, and there was still a part of his heart feeling the swelling tide of sorrow because this man was still his father. All of this left him feeling like he was drowning in melancholy.

At that moment, Emily's words came back to him, and they finally hit the nerve they had been aimed at. Life did indeed have a way of pulling you under, but she was wrong, he realized, or at least it was not completely accurate. It was not a teetering feeling. Harkin was sinking in desolation and choking on apathy. When Emily explained it to him, Harkin did not realize how much it would hurt. He understood now as the pain tightened his throat and constricted his voice.

"Goodbye, son." Eugene said, his voice barely a broken whisper as he had to gasp for breath after those two words.

"Dad?" Was all Harkin could manage in reply, and the weight left on that one word filled the room.

His father smiled weakly, then with every pain and effort clearly displayed, Eugene reached for the machines next to his bed. With the humming stopped, Harkin heard his own sob. Collapsing back into the bed, Eugene closed his eyes. He was still watching his father when one of the other machines began to sound an alarm. Harkin recognized the monitor that was tracking the heartbeat as it alerted him that it could no longer detect one.

Harkin sat there. He was somewhere between stunned and confused. Maybe this is what they mean by in shock, a voice deep in the back of his mind said. He did not know what he had expected to feel at this moment, but he had expected to feel something. The sudden emptiness that hollowed him out had not been a sensation he had accounted for.

"Harkin?" He heard his mother's voice behind him.

"I didn't..." Harkin started as he jumped to his feet, realizing he must have sounded like a guilty child who had broken a lamp with a football in the house.

His mother's reaction startled him. Bea smiled. She walked past him and pressed a button that silenced the alarm. Turning to face him, she still wore the smile but standing this close to her, Harkin could see the pain in her eyes.

"Of course not, dear. He started talking about shutting it off weeks ago. I think he was just waiting on you." She was quiet as if she were waiting for Harkin to respond before finally saying, "You don't have to stay."

"Mom?" Harkin asked, not sure of her meaning.

"If you were staying just to say goodbye. You can go now, honey. It's alright."

"No, mom. I want to stay. Maybe not for the funeral but for you." Bea hugged him, and he asked, "So, now what?"

"Maybe we could catch up?" His mother asked.

"I meant about dad."

"Oh, I need to call Klarissa. She said she could handle the rest." Bea noticed her son's eyebrow quirk at her matter-of-fact tone and guessed the reason, "Dear, he spent his last good weeks preparing me for this, and I've had a few more to mourn when his health took its final turn. Right now, I'm relieved this is over. I will miss him, and I love him, but today is a mercy."

"You're different." That was all Harkin could say in response.

"So are you." His mother remarked evenly, "I remember how you left. Angry and drunk, bound for a fate not too dissimilar to your father's. Now, let's go into the kitchen and talk. I don't like waiting in here. We'll call Klarissa from in there."

Harkin sat quietly at the kitchen table while his mother made the call. Then sitting down on the phone, she smiled at her son.

"So, when did you sober up? As I remember it, you were a pretty heavy drinker for a young man who couldn't even buy beer yet."

The surprise was still in his eyes as Harkin asked, "You knew or even noticed?"

Bea rolled her eyes at her son with that reprimanding smile that only a mother could have, "You really think after marrying your father that I couldn't tell when an alcoholic was trying to hide their habits. Now, I asked a question, young man."

Harkin thought about it. He remembered when he made the decision, but what he could not figure out was how to tell the story. For a hangover, the details were clear, and all shamefully so.

"It was after my nineteenth birthday. It was the first time that Benji and I made introductions."

"Benji?" His mother interrupted.

"You know him as Pastor Ben, I suppose. I had seen him on the grounds before when I would visit Nora, but we had never spoken until that morning."

Harkin fell into silence, and Bea could tell her son was trying to find his next words, so she waited. She could admit that patience was not one of her virtues, but given how long she had been waiting to see if she would ever see her son again, she figured she could work on it.

"I don't know how I got from the bar by the college, but I woke up or rather got woke up at Nora's grave. Benji was prodding me with the handle of his shovel, saying something about having respect. When I told him that she was my sister, he just said that made it worse, and we talked. I realized I had become the thing I hated."

"Your father." Bea offered.

"No. The alcoholic my father was."

Bea lapsed into a sympathetic smile as she looked at her son, "You can admit that you hated your father."

"Maybe it's a very thin distinction, but I didn't hate him. Just a lot of things about him and a lot of the things he did. I don't know, maybe that's not fair, but it's how I felt." Harkin explained.

"I can understand." Bea replied.

"Now it's your turn." He said.

"My turn, what?" His mother challenged.

"You changed, too. Why?"

Bea let go of her breath in an explosive exhalation before saying, "You left. I think that had the most to do with it. I'm not saying any of it was your fault," She clarified as she watched her son's brow furrow, "but it started when I couldn't stand to watch Nora suffer, and when she died, it killed me. After that, your father just completely unraveled, and he wasn't exactly a tightly wound man to start with. You two fought so much I couldn't take it, but then one day I was in this house by myself. You were gone, and your father was always who knows where. I hit my low point then one day, Pastor Ben knocked on the door with an invitation to church and slowly started helping me."

"No surprise that he would be the culprit." Harkin said then mother and son shared a laugh.

"You can say what you want about him, but he is a good man." His mother said when her laughter had subsided.

"I know, even if he is a little shady. I did not realize he was even a pastor until last night. I just always assumed he was retired, and that's why he was the most dedicated groundskeeper I had ever met."

"Well, he is dedicated." Bea agreed.

Harkin chuckled before asking, "So, is that all? He just invited you to church, and you went?"

"No, truthfully, I was never too certain of his interests in inviting your father and me until a few moments ago. I think he came around here because of you."

"I'm sorry." Harkin said with an uncharacteristically roguish grin.

Bea giggled before continuing, "Now that I know that he knew you and how that came to happen, I think he met you first. If I had to guess, he came around here after finding out some of the story from you and tried his best to remedy the pain."

"And how did he do?" Harkin asked.

The sorrow in his mother's smile made Harkin's chest hurt and his heartache when she answered, "Now that you're here, I think he did a pretty good job."

While the medical staff and coroner were still in the other room, Harkin handed his mother a piece of paper, "Maybe better than we give him credit for. I don't know how long I'm staying in town, but you should call sometime."

***

Harkin left the house that night and found himself sitting at the bar. He was surprised when Benji sat next to him.

"Sorry for your loss." Benjamin said as he motioned to the bartender.

Harkin raised an eyebrow, "Are pastors supposed to drink?"

"Who do you think was your father's drinking buddy? We had a lot of church right here at this bar. Besides, it's the indulgence and the seeking refuge in something other than faith that is wrong in drinking. Me being here is more of the 'sheep among the wolves' type of thing. Read the book of Mark sometime, at least the first few chapters. Jesus was the one who was supplying the good wine to keep the party going. People like to argue that water wasn't safe to drink, but He could have just as easily purified the water as He did transform it."

"Benji, if you have any more surprises, please wait until I have a few more beers." Harkin said, taking another drink.

"No more surprises, maybe a sermon or two, though."

"I'm going to need something stronger than beer for that." Harkin said, only half-joking.

"Why are you here drinking tonight? I doubt you're here to pour one out for your old man." Harkin did not answer, and Benjamin sighed, "I'm not here to try to fix anything between you and your dad, but your father was an alcoholic, and I don't want to see you take that path again."

"I don't think it's hereditary." Harkin commented.

"No, but you both have that mindset. Tell me I'm wrong if you want, but just look where you are."

Harkin took a drink, intentionally not looking in Benjamin's direction.

"It's amazing what people are willing to let go in order to punish those who have only ever meant them good."

Harkin sighed, "Really just wanting to make up for all those lost times you could have preached to me, huh?"

Benjamin shrugged, "You ever heard of Barabbas?"

"I don't think you've mentioned him before."

"He was the man that was released so that Christ could be crucified. It was custom to release one prisoner and the ruler of the time wanted to release Christ. See, Barabbas was a criminal. He was a murderer and insurrectionist. He was the one the ruler wanted to see punished, but he gave it to the crowd to decide, and they wanted to see Barabbas released."

"Why?" Harkin asked, genuinely interested.

"Christ challenged the way they did things, and they couldn't have that. They would rather see the murderer go free than be forced to change, and all Christ wanted them to do was care. They gave a pardon to a man that was essentially trying to overthrow their form of government in order to punish the man that was trying to give them salvation."

"What does this have to do with me?"

"You crucified your father when all he wanted was to give you a better life, and when you did that, what do you think you set free? Look at the man you became at the cost of the one you punished."

"I'm starting to think I prefer to drink alone." Harkin responded.

Benjamin sighed, "I'm sure you do. Especially after what I have to say next."

"Don't keep me in suspense, Benji. Spit it out." Harkin muttered as he took another drink.

"Eugene often spoke about the night your sister passed." Benjamin sighed disappointedly at the look on Harkin's face, "Your mother still doesn't have the nerve to tell you. She called after you left this evening to tell me she tried but couldn't do it. I told her I would. Maybe you refuse to believe it, or maybe you don't remember, but your sister was dead before that night."

"What are you talking about?" Harkin asked.

"Your sister was declared brain dead three days earlier than when your father turned off the machines. He always said that back then, they hadn't believed in God or prayed, but he had believed now that at the back of their minds that maybe they were praying for a miracle. He thought you were sleeping; he was going to turn off the machines and let her go peacefully because he thought it would be easier for you that way. When he realized you blamed him, he decided it would be easier to let you."

Harkin took a drink then set the glass back on the bar without looking at Benji. After a few minutes of silence, Benji slipped a bill under his glass then stood.

"I'll be seeing you, Harry."

"Benji." Harkin tipped his glass as Benjamin stood.

✳✳✳

To My Unkindled Love,

There is a caution to be made when amending for change. Do not be overzealous. Yes, you must make direct amends to the peoples you have harmed. There are to be no half efforts with the exception that to make such attempts at amends would injure them or others further.

This is something to make haste of if you truly want to change and recover. "So if you are presenting a sacrifice at the altar in the Temple and you suddenly remember that someone has something against you, leave your sacrifice there at the altar. Go and be reconciled to that person. Then come and offer your sacrifice to God." (Matthew 5:23-24 NLT)

You have to face those fears and those expectations in making your amends. You need to

Faithfully Addicted

forgive anyone who needs your forgiveness. Also, you must sensitively evaluate where making your amends would do more harm than good. Then comes the risk, the familiar part of all of this in a sense. You risk feeling vulnerable and make amends to these individuals. You cannot have change or recovery while you still carry burdens after all.

Evermore,

Your Kindred Heart

Chapter Ten

To whom it may concern,

When someone like you begins to trouble their better angels, they have truly earned that straight jacket. Then again, someone like you doesn't often catch the attention or interest of their better angels. In that alone lies that painful prison of a special kind of purgatory. That state of being in between. The state of passing through endless, countless days of feeling nothing and feeling everything. The state of feeling dead inside and having a racing, raging heart. The state of having a purpose and the state of wanting one. The dream of hope and the reality of being hopelessly adrift.

When someone like you finds that particular piece of hell in the corners of Heaven, pray tell, was it worth it? Was every countless breath up until the moment it hurt to breathe worth the pain? Is that numbing pain comforting at this time? Do you rely so heavily on it to know that your heart is still beating? Pray tell, are you happy to have caught the attention of the better angel that rules over this hell-fired Heaven?

Evermore,

Purgatory's Clock

***

Mrs. Lindsey had time to prepare. It was a sad truth Benjamin understood as he looked at the headstone. It was an impressive piece of India black granite, so well-polished Benjamin could almost see himself in it. It was a married couple's headstone. It had Mrs. Lindsey's name and birth year on it as well. The stone workers would be by tomorrow to carve Mr. Lindsey's death day into it.

Even though Mr. Lindsey's body had not been released yet, Benjamin still gave the headstone a reverent nod as he walked up with his tools. He had just driven the tip of the shovel into the ground of the marked-out plot when he heard the footsteps. Benjamin looked over his shoulder to see Harkin walking toward him. At first, Benjamin was concerned that Harkin might have noticed Benjamin's reluctance, but after really looking at Harkin, Benjamin only felt worried for the man himself.

Harkin was still wearing the same clothes that he had been the night before, and it was obvious that they were slept in. Benjamin did not know where the jacket that Harkin had been wearing was, but the knot of the tie was resting three buttons down the shirt, of which the sleeves were roughly rolled to the elbows. The shirttails hung loosely over the wrinkled trousers, but Benjamin could tell by the fold that the back of the shirt was still tucked in.

"Harry." Benjamin greeted him neutrally.

"Benji. All this time and I thought you were just a gravedigger."

"I don't think anybody is ever just anything. No, the day you pulled me out of that hole, I thought you were saving me, but the more we talked, I realized it was just so I could be here to help save you."

"Let's not go too deep with it," Harkin said with a smirk, "got an extra shovel?"

Benjamin appraised Harkin with a frown before sighing, "Harry, you don't have to."

"You know, I think I do."

Benjamin nodded then handed Harkin one of the shovels.

"All the times I've come here, why didn't you ever say anything?" Harkin asked after a few minutes.

"About your father's drinking? What difference would it have made?"

Harkin laughed bitterly, "Fair point. How about these last couple of times? Why didn't you tell me how bad off he was?"

"I think my question would remain the same." Benjamin said, pausing to watch Harkin dig.

The same bitter laugh escaped Harkin again, and Benjamin could see a genuine hurt in his eyes. It was not anything Benjamin had said. It was the realization of a certain kind of self-loathing that was eating at Harkin. It was the truth that Benjamin was right. It would not have made a difference if Harkin had known. Harkin kept digging, unaware of Benjamin watching him, but he finally stopped to look back at Benjamin.

"Tell me this, why did you never tell me you were a preacher?"

"You didn't want to talk to the preacher. You just wanted to talk to the gravedigger." Benjamin said with a shrug.

"I mean this as a compliment," Harkin said with a sardonic smile, "but you don't seem like a preacher."

As Benjamin started laughing, Harkin resumed digging. Benjamin sat down next to the tarp that already had a reasonable amount of dirt on it.

"It may surprise you to know that it wasn't something I ever intended to be, but much like you, I got tired of walking around dead inside. So, I turned to a faith that is all about the fact that death doesn't win." Benjamin started to explain.

Harkin straightened up, supporting his weight on the shovel as he surveyed Benjamin, "Dead inside? I'm sorry, Benji, but you don't seem the type."

Benjamin's smile faltered, but when it returned, it had become the kind of smile that made Harkin feel miserable. It was not an insincere smile, Harkin could tell that there was real emotion in it, but the overruling emotion in it was pain. Benjamin wore the kind of smile that hurt, and that was hard, but what was worse was the fact that Benjamin wore it comfortably like it was an old friend. In that brief instant, Harkin felt there was a lot more to the pastor turned grave digger than he could have ever imagined.

"Remember when I told you even God needed to rid perfection of loneliness? It doesn't matter how many graves you dig; loneliness isn't something you can bury." Harkin heard the shakiness in Benjamin's voice as he continued, "I lost people growing up. Everybody does. In that regard, I am nothing new, but the two graves I could not dig are where my heart was buried. Post-partum depression wasn't a thing in my day, you know? It was perfectly natural for a woman to have trouble adjusting after childbirth, but nobody understood it like we do now." Benjamin shook his head, still wearing that unbearable smile, "I knew my wife was having trouble sleeping, and I thought that was why she didn't seem happy. Until I came home one day and the house was so quiet. I walked room to room, calling out for her. I think a part of me knew something was wrong."

Harkin looked away in the moment of silence, trying not to see Benjamin wipe away the tears in his eyes.

"I found her in the bathroom. She had run a bath," Benjamin said with steel in his voice, determined to finish, "She and our baby boy were under the surface and had been for some time. No goodbyes, no note, and no way to fix it. Part of me died that day."

"Benji, I'm sorry." Harkin said, "all this time, and I never knew."

"Well, I wasn't about to tell a kid that kind of thing, but yeah, I recognized it in you too, the day you died, and as much as you don't want to hear it or believe it, I recognized it in your father too. Do you want to know why your father's liver was failing? He lost all restraint to his drinking the day you left, and he never got any of it back."

"Are you saying this is my fault?" Harkin asked defensively as he resumed digging.

"Yes, but there is plenty of blame to go around, so don't worry about that. Your mother used to tell me that your father would say he lost both his children. I think he truly believed you were dead to him. The only difference is he didn't have to bury you."

"You don't need to advocate for him." Harkin said, a cold edge creeping into his voice.

"Oh, I'm not." Benjamin declared, "He's dead. It doesn't matter what you've got to say anymore. I'm just trying to get you to live this life before the dead inside of you is all I have to bury."

Harkin stopped, now standing in a hole that came to his knees, to fix Benjamin with an amused smile, "Really think you are going to outlive me?"

"If you don't learn to start leaving some things in that hole, you might as well be digging it for yourself." Benjamin answered flatly.

"This church must really be something if this is how you preach." Harkin remarked.

"Well, I don't have them dig their own graves usually." Benjamin admitted.

"Too bad," Harkin said with another laugh, "it really helps with the hard sell."

"They don't always need the hard sell. Not everyone needs the extra help making good choices that you do."

Harkin kept digging quietly while Benjamin sat there watching, then Harkin stopped when he was standing in a squared-off hole just past his waist. He looked at Benjamin then shook his head.

"What?" Benjamin asked.

"How did you do it? You say you found faith. That's great and all. I'll give you that it helps some people, but you said you found it. That means you went looking for it. What made you go looking?"

This time when Benjamin smiled, there was genuine happiness in his eyes with a mild surprise, "I knew you were a smart kid. I was wondering when you would get there. My daughter was the reason I started looking."

Another shocking expression possessed Harkin's features, "Daughter?"

"The young lady, you saw here the other day. That is my daughter Klarissa."

When Benjamin said it, the moment of déjà vu came over him again, and Harkin made the connection finally.

"Wait, the nurse. That's your daughter?" Harkin asked.

"Yes. I told you I died that day, and I didn't lie," Benjamin began, "but when my little girl got off the school bus and ran across the yard, I accepted I still had responsibilities."

"You just kept breathing." Harkin added with a nod of his head.

"Precisely. I've never asked her if she felt neglected growing up. I've been too ashamed because I'm sure she did. I did all the things I was supposed to do, and that was all I was doing. I doubt she felt loved because I wasn't giving any."

"Seems like she turned out alright." Harkin offered.

"To no credit of mine. She was twelve years old; it was about four years after her mother left us. I got a call from the school; child protective services had been called and would like to speak to me." Benjamin stopped to shake his head with a bitter smile, "One of the teachers that did not know all the details of my wife's passing but had known Klarissa since she had started school was beginning to see changes in her that she thought were signs of abuse." Benjamin held up a hand in response to Harkin's indignant expression, "Looking back, she wasn't wrong. I was emotionally abusive to my daughter by not living for her."

"But they didn't take her away from you, did they? They couldn't have." Harkin rambled in stunned disbelief.

"No, once we all sat down and talked through it, they realized I just needed a little help to get back on track. The social worker there from child services recommended all kinds of therapy and counseling options to help me with my job and Klarissa. But that teacher, once she knew the story, she invited me to this very church where she played the piano for the congregation on Sunday mornings. So, I came looking for answers."

"And you found them?" Harkin asked.

"I did." Benjamin answered.

"What were the answers?"

"I can't tell you that. See, everyone has different questions. The best I can do is help show you where to look."

"Ever the preacher, Benji. All talk until it's time to actually say something." Harkin muttered as he started digging again.

Benjamin laughed, taking no offense at the comment, "You know much of your Scripture, Harry?"

"No." Harkin replied flatly.

"Then let me tell you a story. You do know who Jesus is, right?" Benjamin chuckled as Harkin shot him a look, "Well, one of Jesus' followers had that just keep breathing moment. He was the one out to prove them all wrong, you know the type, everyone else may fail, but he was not about to."

"Let me guess, he screwed up." Harkin interrupted in a bored tone.

"Royally." Benjamin answered before continuing, "I'm talking about the one who denied Christ. Peter was his name, just in case you were curious. But Peter was the one to turn around and say 'no, I don't know that guy' three different times as Christ was being arrested, prosecuted, and crucified. Do you know what he did next?"

"Killed himself." Harkin guessed with a disinterested shrug as he kept digging.

"No, that was one of the others. Peter went fishing." Benjamin smiled as Harkin paused for the briefest of seconds to look at him and Benjamin continued, "Yeah, I'm serious. The guy went fishing, but that was because he was giving up. He was going back to what he knew how to do and what he thought he was good at and what he had been doing before Christ made an appearance in his life. The really telling thing about all of it, though, he wasn't any good at it."

Harkin leaned his shovel against the hole he was digging and sat on the edge with his legs hanging into the fresh earth. He sighed as he eyed Benjamin before he finally spoke.

"Benji, I assume you are getting to a point. Is there any way to speed it up?" Harkin asked.

Benjamin gestured for Harkin to move his legs as he settled into the grave to start digging as he spoke, "Maybe you could answer a few questions instead of heckling an old preacher, and things might go faster."

"Sorry." Harkin replied sincerely.

"Don't worry about it. Anyway, Jesus appeared to them after they had been fishing all night, and they hadn't caught a thing. You put the worst fisherman you know on a boat for a night, and you know he is at least going to catch something. Now you do the same thing with a guy that used to do it for a living, and you have much higher expectations. Fishing had been Peter's livelihood, and he didn't even catch one fish."

"Okay, I get it. He sucked at his job." Harkin interrupted and caught Benjamin's raised eyebrow, "Sorry."

"Harry, you're missing my point. I repeat that not to tell you he was horrible at his job, but when you're a member of the walking dead that just keeps breathing, you aren't doing the job like you used to." Harkin grunted with a shake of his head, "Now you're getting there." Benjamin heckled in return.

"I thought pastors were supposed to be compassionate and understanding?" Harkin barbed.

"You're a special case." Benjamin quipped, "Harry, Peter could not even return to his livelihood because he was carrying the pain he had, but when Jesus showed up, Peter kept trying desperately to fix it."

"Could you define desperately for those of us who don't know the story?" Harkin interjected.

"Sure, as long as they are patient in letting me get to the point. When Peter realized it was Jesus calling to them from the shore, he threw himself overboard and swam to the shore just to get to him, and I know you think that doesn't seem so bad, but scripture says the guys in the boat reached the shore about the same time, so it's not like he did things any faster. He could have just stayed in the boat. The next thing he did, and I forgot to mention this part, was before they came to shore, Jesus told them where to cast their nets, so they had fish when they reached the shore, but when Jesus asked them to bring some of their fish, Peter himself climbed back into the boat to drag that net, which I imagine was rather heavy, to the shore by himself. He was trying to prove himself to make up for what he had done."

"Did it work?" Harkin asked.

Benjamin stopped digging to look into Harkin's eyes, "That's the point, Harry. He didn't have to do any of that. Jesus showed up on that shore because he did not want Peter to stop living. He was there to encourage him, not give him a chance to fix something. Jesus pulled Peter aside on that shore in that early morning light to ask him one question the same amount of times that Peter had denied Him. Do you love me? Then Christ told Peter to get to work. He still had a purpose and a plan. He couldn't just go hide out on a boat and stop living."

"Benji, I don't own a boat." Harkin said with a wry smile.

"And I don't think you can fish either, but you stopped living just the same, and I don't think you want the answers that you will find at the bottom of this grave if you don't start finding a reason to live. Now go, you've helped me enough, and you've paid your respects to your old man. I know you don't plan on being here for the funeral, and I'll make sure your mother understands."

"She does, and she has my number. I told her I would do a better job coming around." Harkin replied.

"Good. You take care, Harry." Benjamin said, reaching out his hand to shake Harkin's.

"You too, Benji. And, thank you." Harkin replied, grasping the man's outstretched hand.

***

His father had finally given up, and Harkin found his mind focusing on another worry. Emily had stopped calling or answering his calls after the first night. Her voicemail was full, and no longer taking messages. He decided he needed to know why.

Rosie was at the counter when he walked in, and she glared at him. Before he could say anything, she placed a placard on the counter. He half glanced down at it and saw the words "refuse service."

Harkin chuckled in bewilderment, "What's this about, Rosie?"

"You know." She declared, crossing her arms and her eyes narrowing.

"I assure you, I don't." He insisted.

"She relapsed," Rosie asserted, "because of you."

"When? Wait! What? Because of me?" Harkin stammered.

For the first time, Rosie's eyes softened, and her voice had lost most of its icy tone, "You really don't know?" She asked.

"No!" Harkin's voice cracked, causing a few of the patrons to look in their direction, but he ignored them.

Placing his hands on the counter, trying to control himself, "I just got back into town. She hasn't answered my calls for two days."

Rosie sighed, "She's back in the clinic. Ray found her. She had shot up."

Rosie was speaking in very clipped sentences, and Harkin realized that she did not want to be the one telling him any of this.

"Thank you." He relented, "I will call your husband and let you get back to work."

She moved the little sign off the counter, "Did you want something?" She asked, and Harkin knew that was as close as he was going to get to an apology.

"No." He said politely as he turned on his heels.

"Wait!" Rosie called out behind him.

When Harkin turned to face her again, she gestured to one of the other girls to take the counter as she took off her apron.

"Let's talk outside." She said, in a much softer voice than she had used before as she walked past him to the door.

Harkin fell into step behind her without a word, and he hoped without too much of a frown on his face. Outside, she pulled a chair from an empty table and gestured for him to sit across from her.

"You know it was never anything against you personally, don't you?"

"Ma'am?" Harkin asked.

"I know that you know some of Emilia's past. I know that you know she was an addict. Do you know why it is discouraged for addicts to have relationships?"

Harkin sat forward-leaning his elbows on the table, "Emily said relationships could cause a relapse. I never pushed her into this."

"I know, young man. Do you know why they trigger a relapse? What is really happening?" Rosie pressed.

"No, I don't." Harkin admitted, "Would you like to enlighten me?"

"Watch your tone, and I'm going to do just that. Although some of it may not seem like a big deal, you need to understand that an addict's brain has been chemically compromised. The year that is recommended is to give the brain time to readjust and become chemically and hormonally balanced."

"Okay, I didn't know the exact reason, but I understand that, and I take it seriously."

"No, you still don't understand. When a recovering addict interacts with someone inside of that year window, the chemical reactions in their brain are not normalized yet." Rosie paused, then gave Harkin a sigh, "Harkin."

Harkin was looking at her, but at this, he sat up, giving her a curious look.

"Did you feel that?" Rosie asked.

"What?"

"That little spark in the back of your mind because I said your name. That is a chemical response. There are several neuroscience journals and psychology studies that explain how someone reacts when someone says their name. Affections, attractions, or even a sense of self-worth or value can be assigned by hearing a name."

"Are you saying this is my fault because I said her name?" Harkin asked.

"No, you're not listening." Rosie asserted, "The name was an example of the small things you don't realize have an effect on her. Maybe things she didn't even fully grasp how they would affect her. Simple things you said or maybe the fact that you would be at her place of employment or not. There are several things you were doing that were harmless under normal circumstances but with Emily led to this."

"So, what are you saying?" Harkin asked.

"I'm not going to tell you to stay away from her, but from here on, you need to be careful. If she gets clean again, understand this starts over from day one.

Every small thing could have a tremendous emotional and mental impact. You need to be aware of that."

"I understand."

"I hope so. Now, my husband is at the church if you still want to talk to him."

"Thank you, ma'am." Harkin replied.

***

Harkin saw Pastor Ray sitting in the front pew with his elbows resting on thighs and his head down as he waited on Harkin. Harkin felt momentarily guilty for his conduct on the phone call, but his need to know what happened drove it back.

"How is she?" Harkin asked as he rounded the pew coming out of the center aisle to sit next to the pastor.

"Stable." Ray said gruffly.

"What does that mean?" The anger rising in Harkin's voice again.

Ray's eyes flashed with a dangerous fury, "Understand, it only takes one time, and she still has to go through withdrawal, and now she has to start all over on a struggle to stay clean. The high is not a distant memory anymore! It's fresh! Now, she has to fight that much harder." He finished in a cold whisper.

Harkin nodded, not that the pastor was looking at him anymore, "So, what happens now?"

"The first time she was going through rehabilitation, the church paid for it with the second chance fund. It is what we use to get recovering addicts the help they need. Now... I have to try to petition the church to use it again for Emilia, and I will tell you now as much as everyone likes her. We do have rules in place for that fund, so it is not likely."

"Don't worry about the money. I will cover the cost." Harkin inserted.

At this, the pastor who had resumed resting on his elbows again looked back over his shoulder at Harkin, "Son, it isn't cheap."

"I can afford it."

The pastor grunted, "Why?"

"I would think a man in your professional could believe in a man wanting to do the right thing."

"Oh, it's easy for me to believe that people want to, but rarely is it for the right reasons. So, why?"

Harkin let out a breath as if preparing for a test of endurance, "Although I don't believe I am solely responsible for her relapse, I know she did warn me of the dangers to her. I just want to help."

"I suppose this is where I tell you that you've done enough and let you walk away. Let you wash your hands of the whole thing and be entirely content to think you tried, right?"

"Your cynicism aside, you can attempt to appease me all you like. I'm not walking away. It would just be easier if I didn't have to fight you too."

"Do you mean that, young man?"

"Yes, sir, I do. But, can I ask, why is it so important to you?"

There was a suspicious squint to Ray's gaze, "What do you mean?"

"Why is Emily so important to you?"

"RJ." Ray answered simply.

Harkin could tell that Ray was trying to think of what to say next, so he waited. The stillness of the church settled around them, and for the first time in days, Harkin felt like he could breathe until Ray cleared his throat. That simple act caused Harkin's breath to bury itself in his chest, the anticipation building so that it was painful to exhale.

"Raymond Junior. We called him RJ, and what I'm about to tell you about him Emily doesn't know."

"Did Emily know your son?" Harkin interrupted.

"I'm not sure she knows I had a son." Harkin was about to ask why it was relevant before his mind registered Ray's use of the past tense. Ray seemed to recognize the realization in Harkin's eyes because he continued, "He was taken home about a year ago now. He was twenty-two, working on getting his degree and teaching history. He had a real passion for it."

Darren Finney

Ray trailed off as he lost himself in the memory while Harkin sat there, his mind reeling with more questions than he had the courage to ask. The first and foremost was why Ray was telling him about his son as a way to explain how he felt about Emily. Harkin's mind was already building the scenario that may be Emily was really his daughter-in-law. Had the death of RJ been what had pushed her over the edge then forced her to get clean? No, he told himself, Ray had just said that Emily did not even know RJ. Then why tell him any of this? Harkin kept asking himself as he tried to remember if Emily had ever told him how she had even met Ray or how she had ended up in the hospital to start with.

"Has Emily ever told you how she ended up in the hospital?" Ray's voice broke into and repeated Harkin's thoughts.

"I know she overdosed, but no, she didn't."

Ray nodded, "That is true enough. Emily did overdose, and when she did, she was not alone. She was with a friend, Misty, another addict, who drove her to the hospital. I found out recently that the other young lady left Emily in the parking lot because she was high as well. This other young lady was concerned about the hospital staff noticing, so she dumped Emily and left. On her way from the hospital, this other young woman hit my son as they were going through an intersection. He was declared dead at the scene."

Ray's voice had slipped into a monotone recital of the facts as he distanced himself from the emotions within. It was a tactic Harkin recognized well.

"And she doesn't know?" Harkin asked.

Ray shook his head, "No, she does not. Nor, do I believe, does my wife. The other young lady reached out to make amends, and my wife did listen to her. As my wife later recounted the details to me, I began to fit the pieces together with Emily's story." Harkin watched as Ray's eyes filled with tears and a wave of undirected anger, "I'm not sure I could have forgiven her or helped her had I known from the start, and I ask God to forgive me for it, but when I met Emily I could see the terrified, broken woman, not the addict. I couldn't be angry with her, and I couldn't abandon her." Ray stopped to see a smirk on Harkin's lips, "If you find something funny in all this, I would love to hear because it has been a year, and I haven't found anything funny."

"No, sir, it reminded me of something I heard recently. If you had crucified her, who would you have set free? Look at the man you could become versus the one you could punish."

Ray's gaze shifted from irritation to curiosity, "That's an interesting perspective. Where did you get it?"

"From a gravedigger talking about Barabbas, I think that was the name." Harkin replied uncertainly.

Ray nodded, "Ah, yes. Barabbas is correct." Ray chuckled before he spoke again, "And I see your point, well a point in what you're trying to say anyway I don't know if it's the one you intended. The world released Barabbas in order to crucify Christ, but even from the cross, Christ reached out to another criminal hanging there. Did you know that?" Harkin shook his head in response, "As Christ hung there dying for the sins of the world, a criminal hanging next to him asked Christ to remember him when he came back, and Christ told him he would be with Him in paradise. One criminal was set free, and another was saved in the process it took to crucify Christ. Hmm."

"You lost me, Pastor. I was just trying to point out that maybe Emily needed to be set free for your son to fulfill his purpose." Harkin interjected.

"Oh, I got that." Ray said with a smile toward Harkin, "But, and please don't think I consider you or Miss Emily criminals any more than I do the rest of us, my way of looking at it has a way of setting two free, not just the one."

Harkin shook his head, "I really need to stop hanging around you preacher types. I am not looking to be saved."

"Yet, here you are."

"Here I am." Harkin agreed, "So, you won't abandon her?"

"No, but I don't think I can risk making it worse and hurting her by telling her the truth."

"And when she finds out? Or your wife does?" Harkin pressed.

"They don't need to."

"That may be true, but they will. If not from you, then from this Misty, and which do you think will do more damage? Right now, it might be your best option to start over while she's rebuilding."

"I can't." Ray admitted.

"I could do it?" Harkin offered hesitantly.

Ray eyed him with speculative and suspicious appreciation, "Why would you be willing to do that?"

Harkin shrugged as he thought about it, "Like you said. I got to meet the woman, not the addict, and much like you, I saw she is something special." This time Ray smiled, but before he could say anything, Harkin continued, "Could I see her?"

Ray's smile faltered slightly but only to slip into that pastorally compassionate gaze, "She is allowed visitors. That being said, you aren't on any acceptable visitors list, and you need to understand the adverse effects your visits could have on her recovery." Harkin started to object, but Ray waved him off, "However, I am willing to call the clinic and have you placed on the visitor's list as long as your visits do not seem to have negative effects."

"Thank you, sir."

"Of course. I will call you when you can go." Harkin made to stand, but Ray stopped him, holding out a set of keys, "By the way, your car is in the back parking lot. I checked the registration when we found Emily."

Harkin took the keys without responding, a guilty expression crossing his features, only briefing as he turned to leave.

**

Sitting in his car outside of his apartment thinking about the conversation he had with Ray, Harkin heard his cellphone vibrate. Reaching for it, he was confused when it the screen remained locked, but he still could still hear the buzzing. That was when he realized there was another phone in the passenger seat. Without thinking, and mostly out of habit, Harkin grabbed the phone and swiped the screen to accept the call. The screen filled with the picture of a woman with short hair and piercing green eyes. Her smile fell, and Harkin realized he had answered a video call.

"Are you Mr. Damaged Goods? Where's Emily?" The woman chirped suspiciously.

"Damaged goods?" Harkin repeated questioningly.

"That's a yes." The woman said with a smirk, then repeated, "Where's Emily?"

Harkin took a deep breath, "She relapsed. I just found her phone."

"What happened?" The woman asked. For the first time, Harkin saw the timer in the corner of the screen and wondered if he had enough time for this conversation.

"I don't know exactly. I was out of town and just found out for myself this morning." Hazarding a guess, Harkin asked, "Misty?"

"Yes. Did she tell you about me?" Misty asked, only slightly surprised.

"No, her pastor or sponsor, whatever he is did." Harkin answered.

"Oh." She replied, and Harkin could see hurt in her features.

He could not explain why but he felt the need to comfort her, "In her defense, she really hasn't told me much other than she was recovering. I don't think she had been ready to share all the details with me yet. However, I have to assume from the damaged goods comment that I am at a disadvantage in that regard."

Misty smiled with a small shake of her head, "Not so much. She just told me you didn't run screaming when she told you she was an addict, and the fact that you seem to have no problem chatting on a prison video call does kind of confirm it."

Harkin laughed, "That's fair. Umm, listen, I'm going to go see Emily soon, but there is something that

I need to talk to you about first that might require more time than this call has left. Are you allowed visitors?"

Harkin could not read the reaction in her eyes. Was it suspicious or just curiosity as she answered, "Yes. I am."

***

To My Unkindled Love,

Ideally, by now, you are starting to feel some semblance of peace. You've made a decision to have a relationship with God that is a slow fight of surrender to overcome yourself. In doing so, you examined yourself and made amends for the harm you have caused through wrongdoings and shortcomings.

Now, you must continue to make that progress by continually taking that personal inventory, and when you are in the wrong, promptly admit it. Carry no more shame of your past but do not forget what brought you here.

"Because of the privilege and authority God has given me, I give you this warning; don't think you are better than you really are. Be honest in your evaluation of yourselves, measuring yourselves by the faith God has given us." (Romans 12:3 NLT)

Faithfully Addicted

You must make it an honest, humble habit to reassess yourself for any future wrongs you may commit as you strive towards better behavior, and you have to confess your wrongs as soon as you become aware of them. You can only have change if it remains a constant effort.

Evermore,

Your Kindred Heart

Chapter Eleven

To Whom It May Concern;

Even regret likes keepsakes. Remorse loves a good memory. It is only natural that your mistakes would give them plenty of both. It is expected that you couldn't let go of the pain, dearest. That is why regret and remorse refuse to let you go. You've given them too much to work with. With all of this thinking, you could live past those painful moments. Pray tell, was it worth it?

I suppose not if you're talking to me again. Don't worry, I'm not offended that you only look to me when the voices in your own head get to be too much. Don't flatter yourself into thinking it a privilege or honor, mind *you. I just personally take great satisfaction in reminding you that you still aren't any better than your last mistake.*

Evermore,

Error's Fault

***

Harkin watched as the guard lead Misty to the table in the visitor's lounge, making the realization that Misty possessed the same kind of comfortable beauty as Emily. Neither woman would claim that they were beautiful, but each had that unnamable quality to captivate a room. She slid into the chair and waited as the guard secured her wrist to the table, giving Harkin an uneasy smile.

"So?" She prompted, and Harkin could hear the nervousness in her voice, "You said this had to do with Emily."

"I know what happened the night you were arrested, and she was committed to the hospital." Harkin began.

"You mean leaving her on the curb and the car accident?" She asked.

"Yes, but it's more than that. You called the mother of the young man to make amends, correct?"

Harkin saw the curious quirk of her eyebrow again as she said, "Yes."

"Her name was Rosie Scott. Her husband is Pastor Raymond Scott, the church of the second chance fund that paid for Emily's first trip to rehab." Misty's eyes widened, and Harkin continued, "Okay, so you didn't know either. That's part of what I wanted to know."

"What else did you want to know?" Misty asked, and there was no hiding the fear in her voice now.

"Should Emily know?" Harkin asked.

Misty did not immediately answer. Harkin watched her look down at the table and take a deep breath, then when she looked back up at him, he could see the tears building in her eyes.

"She came to see me," Misty said, her voice breaking, "did I do this to her? Did they find out when she came to see me? Did I hurt her?"

Harkin instinctively reached out to grasp her hands to comfort her when he saw the guard make to step toward him.

"Sorry," Harkin said to the guard pulling his hands back before focusing on Misty again, "Mrs. Scott does not know the connection you have to Emily. Ray does, and he has been too afraid to tell her the truth because he doesn't want to risk her recovery. You're not to blame for what happened. I am here because you're in her situation, and I need to know if she needs to know this time why people are helping her. You didn't endanger her. I need to know if I'm going too."

Not able to wipe away the tears, Misty blinked several times to clear her vision before smiling at him, "The fact that you think enough to ask makes me think that you are not likely to, but I understand what you're really asking. You want to know if I thought I could handle that kind of information if I were in her shoes?" Harkin nodded, "I don't know. Ray? Is he still willing to help her?"

"Yes, he is."

"Is the church going to pay for her rehab again?" This time Harkin could hear the surprise in her curiosity.

"No." Harkin answered, "The way the fund is arranged, they aren't likely to pay for someone to go through it again if they relapse, but the cost isn't going to be a problem. She will be able to stay."

Misty quirked an eyebrow, her voice drawing out each syllable as she asked, "Are you paying for her rehab?"

"As far as she will know, it was covered in a donation to the church. Is that a problem?"

"No," She said, shaking her head, "just interesting. Now, for what you asked, I think you're right. She probably does need to know, and sooner, the better. If you wait until she gets out again, that kind of emotional weight could trigger another relapse, but if you do it while she is still in the clinic, it will force her to process it in a less self-destructive way. But you don't know what triggered it this time?" Misty added.

"No, I'm going to go see her later today. I'm hoping to find out. Would you like for me to tell her you said hi?"

"Please." Misty paused to bite her lip then gave him an embarrassed smile, "I know this seems like it's a little late to be asking, but I don't think I should keep calling you Mr. Damaged Goods. What is your name?"

He laughed, "It's Harkin."

"Well, Harkin. I have two favors to ask of you." He gestured for her to continue, "First, I would really like it if you kept me updated on her progress. If you don't want to keep visiting me in person, that paper on the table tells you how to arrange the same kind of video call you answered a couple of days ago."

Harkin picked up the piece of paper and stuck it in his jeans pocket, "I can do that. What's the second thing?"

"You've met the Scotts. Do you think they will ever forgive me?" Seeing the expression on Harkin's face, Misty quickly added, "If it makes you uncomfortable, you don't have to answer."

"No, it's not that. I just don't know how I am supposed to answer that. Ray, I think he could forgive you. He just hasn't been given the opportunity. His struggle with finding out who Emily really is has helped him with that. As for Rosie?" Harkin shrugged, "She blames me for Emily relapsing, and I doubt she'll ever forgive me for that. That is a woman who believes in leaving burnt bridges alone, but I don't think you should hold your entire recovery process around her." Misty's eyes narrowed, giving him a searching look, so Harkin continued, "I've learned a lot about addiction and dependency lately, and one thing I've learned is you have to get past yourself before you worry about making anyone else your obstacle. You ask if they will ever forgive you. Will you ever forgive you for it?"

Misty was nodding along with Harkin, not meeting his eyes, "I think you're a good person for Em to have in her corner." She said, avoiding addressing his question, "Thank you."

"Of course." Harkin said, standing as the guard started toward them to take Misty back.

***

When Emily walked back to her room after a group counseling session, she froze in the door. Sitting in a chair at the little table in her room and flipping through one of her notebooks was Harkin. It was hard to discern his emotion because she was too distracted by how much in disarray his appearance seemed. A tie was loosened around his neck with the top button of his shirt undone. His sleeves were rolled past his elbows in a very roughly handled manner. His suit jacket was on the floor, wadded up against one of the chair legs. And the way his shirttails were hanging out of his jeans was not meant to be a fashion statement, but more of a could not be bothered to care attitude. She could tell that he had started the day trying to make an effort, but it had failed sometime earlier. When he looked up to see her, however, he still smiled warmly.

"I wasn't sure at first that they would let me visit."

"How did you get in here?" She asked.

Harkin smiled guiltily, "I might have gotten Pastor Ray to vouch for me."

"Resourceful. I'm not sure if I should be impressed you would do something so sweet or worried that you would do something so stalkerish."

"I'll accept a combination of both."

They laughed together but if fell back into an awkward silence. Emily stepped a little closer into the room, but she did not approach the table where he was sitting.

"You don't want me here, do you?" Harkin asked her.

"No, it's not that. I am glad to see you. I'm just sorry."

"Can you tell me why?" He asked calmly.

"I would think that would be obvious."

He frowned at her, "I don't mean why you're sorry. I know you are not three years old. I'm not scolding you." She gave him that whimsical smile of hers again at this, "Can you tell me why you did it? Was it something I did?"

"Somebody thinks an awful lot of themselves." Emily attempted at humor, but Harkin's frown remained.

Emily crossed the room then sat down in the other chair. She did not speak for a few minutes but instead became increasingly focused on her hands as she picked at the end of her nails. When she finally looked up, she saw Harkin sitting there patiently waiting on her.

"It wasn't you." Emily admitted.

Harkin only slowly nodded.

"I don't do good with funerals or death, really. I'm sorry about your dad, by the way."

Again, Harkin said nothing but seemed to brush off her condolences as he only quirked an eyebrow at this.

Emily pointed a finger at him, "Oh, shut up!" She said, amused, "I know what you're thinking."

Harkin wordlessly made a defensive flourish of his hand.

"Okay, please say something." Emily pleaded.

Harkin sighed, "I'm sorry. I really am trying to understand. Why are funerals so hard for you?"

"And I appreciate that. I really do. It's just hard to talk about." Emily took a deep breath, steeling herself, "I had a son. His name was Spencer. He died just before turning four months. SIDS. One morning, I went to his crib, and he had stopped breathing during the night."

"I'm so sorry." Harkin said sincerely.

"I was nineteen, and his father was a deadbeat. I didn't even list him on the birth certificate. But we had a little service for him, and it was probably only a few weeks later I started drinking."

"And that's where the cycle started." Harkin finished.

Emily nodded, "I just kept trying to dull the pain. I would try anything then. A friend is the one who introduced me to heroin the first time. That was different. I was happy for the first time in a long time."

Harkin started to raise his eyebrow again, and Emily shook her head.

"I know it wasn't real. They explain that all here." She said, waving her hand around, gesturing to her surroundings, "They talk about how drugs like that affect the pleasure centers of the brain. Some of the people in here say it's better than really good sex but, really it's different."

Harkin snorted before he could stop himself.

Emily smiled, "I could see where this could get awkward and hilarious, but I am not about to describe to you the merits of which is better sex or drugs. That would be just too much."

Harkin raised his hands defensively with a wide grin, "I have always been a 'hugs, not drugs' guy, myself."

Emily started laughing, bringing a hand up to cover her mouth, "Cute." She said when she finally got control of herself.

"Anyway," Harkin said, looking around casually, "We were talking about your search for pleasure and happiness."

"It sounds so wrong when you say it like that." Emily said, frowning at him.

Harkin shrugged with a mischievous grin.

"Anyway." Emily drawled, "Maybe happy isn't the right word, but I felt good. This is where the stories all sound the same." Emily sighed, "I was using more and more just to keep feeling that way. Snorting and smoking it. Then I tried shooting it."

"Then what happened?"

"I overdosed." Emily answered as she reached into the back pocket of her jeans then held up a spoon, "This is the last one."

"You lost me." Harkin remarked

"My grandmother left me her silver cutlery. It was valuable. I pawned most of it for money, and I kept the spoons. This is the last one that is not ruined."

"Interesting keepsake."

"It's a horrible reminder." She responded.

"Can I make a suggestion?"

This time she quirked an eyebrow at him, suspiciously, "What?"

"Let's make it a promise."

"You lost me." She mimicked.

"We will use that spoon like crazy on your victory ice cream when you get out of here."

"Are you serious?"

"I never joke about Rocky Road."

This time she giggled, "Nice! I meant about being around when I get released?"

"What are friends for?" Harkin asked softly.

"Just friends?" Emily asked.

"I think your recovery requires it, but that's alright. I'm a patient man when I need to be."

"Again, I ask. Do you mean that?" Emily asked, her blue eyes directly meeting his for the first time since entering the room.

"I do, but I do have a question?"

"What?" Emily asked cautiously.

"Does this mean I still fall into that Mr. Damaged Goods category?" Emily's jaw dropped, and Harkin chuckled, "I may have met Misty. You left your phone in my car. She says hi."

Emily dropped her face into her hands, and Harkin heard her mutter a rather choice expletive or two before sitting bolt upright with her hands over her mouth, and a horrified guilty expression on her face, "Sorry, that just slipped out."

"I'm not judging." Harkin said with a grin.

"I completely forgot about that call. How was she?"

"Worried about you. I told her I would keep her up to date as long as you would let me."

"Thank you."

"You're welcome," Harkin replied, "but you still haven't answered my question."

Emily groaned, "She called you that, not me. Just point of fact." Harkin laughed again before she continued, "She wondered why a decent guy wouldn't run after finding out about my past. Obviously, since you are having so much fun with this right now, we can only establish you are not a decent guy." She said teasingly.

Harkin mockingly put a hand to his chest, "Well played."

They drifted into a silence that was not as uncomfortable as it was before, but it was still far from easy. Emily sat watching him, and she could tell he had something more to say, but she was too anxious to ask him what it was. She wondered what he really thought of her now. She questioned if he really intended to come back. She questioned why he was there at all. Emily could not understand the thoughts that Harkin must have been thinking, but she was afraid to ask him to explain them.

"When I found out you had been readmitted," He startled her as he spoke in an unsteady voice, "I ended up speaking with Ray, and I found out something that I really don't know if I should tell you."

"What?" She asked cautiously.

Seeming to ignore her, Harkin continued in the same shaky voice, "I asked Misty if I should, and she thought now that you would be forced to deal with it in a healthy way, it would be best. But I still don't know if I want to tell you."

"Harkin, tell me what?" She pressed.

"The young man that Misty hit when she left the hospital...was Ray's son." Harkin finished with a sigh, unsure of her reaction.

Emily dropped her face in her hands again, and Harkin heard her mumbled through her fingers, "How could they not tell me?"

"When Ray figured it out, it was after you had gone through the program the first time. Rosie still doesn't know." Emily's head shot up to look at Harkin, and he saw the tears streaking her cheek, "When he found out, he was afraid of the damage it would do to you, so he didn't say anything to you or to Rosie. In fact,

I was the one to tell Misty when I asked if you should know. You should know they all still support you."

"How?" She asked.

"I think there is something in that book you all like about forgiveness." Harkin said.

Emily gave him a disapproving scowl, "I'm serious. You shouldn't be so disrespectful just because you don't believe it."

Harkin shook his head before saying in a voice that carried an edge, "You stumbled. Even Jesus forgave the guy that did that. He came back to ask him repeatedly if he loved Him just to make the point that He still cared for the guy." Emily smiled, causing Harkin to pause, "What?"

"Nothing. It's kind of cute watching you talk like you get it."

Harkin shrugged, "Turns out I know a guy."

"Thank you." Emily said with a cautious smile.

Harkin returned her smile, "Can I ask you something?"

"Sure?"

"What is this?" Harkin asked, holding up the notebook he had been reading from when she had come back to the room.

Realizing what Harkin had been reading, Emily made to pull it away from him, but he quickly slid it out of her grasp then sat it back on the table.

She sighed reluctantly, "One of the exercises they encourage here is keeping a journal or a diary. I think it is meant to help mark progress, but it doesn't always feel that way."

"But these are letters." Harkin observed.

"Writing letters was easier for me than just keeping a journal, so I wrote letters."

"Very interesting letters. To whom it may concern? My unkindled love? Condemned warden? Kindred Heart? I don't get it."

She smiled guiltily, "Can I explain another time."

"Of course. As long as I can visit another time."

A little of the guilt left her smile, "Of course."

***

After leaving the clinic, Harkin had driven out to the little church to find Benji. It was not a planned visit, but he had learned that more often than not, he would be able to find him working the grounds. Harkin felt a little guilty for having missed his father's funeral only to return so soon, but if Benji judged him for it, the old man did not let it show. They had sat on the front steps of the church to talk, and Harkin admitted to himself that it was strange to carry on a conversation with the man when it was not over a headstone. Harkin had proceeded to tell Benji everything that had happened after returning, and Benji listened patiently, never interrupting nor offering any prompting, but he had let Harkin tell the story in his own way and in his own time.

Until finally, Harkin looked over at the man then asked, "What am I doing, Benji?"

"I dare say, I think you're doing the right thing." Benji replied.

"What? Were you listening? She may have said that I wasn't the reason she ended up there again, but I certainly didn't help her avoid it." Harkin protested.

"But," Benji said, leaning back on the stairs to rest his back against the door, he had sat one stair above Harkin, but this motion put them sitting where they could meet each other's eyes levelly, "neither did you abandon her or push her to it."

"This wasn't the way it was supposed to go." Harkin remarked feebly.

"You know that for a fact, do you?" Benji asked in a jovial yet reprimanding tone.

"What do you mean?" Harkin asked suspiciously.

Benji smiled at Harkin as he said, "It's funny the way God can work a man's plans from time to time. It can leave a man carrying on a full conversation with an animal like it's a normal thing."

Harkin raised an eyebrow as he responded, "I get this is about to lead to another one of your Bible stories, no doubt, but I'll bite. What are you talking about?"

"A guy named Balaam and his donkey. See here, this guy was riding his donkey, and three different times it misbehaves, so naturally, he uses his stick and corrects it. After the third time, the donkey asks Balaam why."

"Benji, if I didn't know better, I'd accuse you of making this up just to screw with me." Harkin admitted.

"Read your Bible, Harry. It's full of the weird and unbelievable."

"See," Harkin declared with a smile, "you use the word unbelievable to describe it then wonder why I'm not a big believer."

Benji frowned at Harkin before replying testily, "That's a weak argument. You claim not to believe in love either, but here you are playing digital matchmaker."

"I make one joke about silver singles, and now you refuse to accept my profession as legitimate." Harkin mumbled wearily.

Benji smiled at their familiar joke, glad to see some of the old Harkin return, then he said, "I'll accept your profession when you accept mine."

"Fair enough," Harkin said with a shrug mirroring Benji's smile, "so this Balaam guy. I'm guessing he freaked out?"

"No," Benji replied, "he accused it of making a mockery of him then told it that if he had had a sword, he would have killed it."

"Bet that went over well." Harkin muttered.

Ignoring the interruption, Benji continued, "the donkey replied by pointing out that Balaam had ridden it all his life, and it hadn't done this kind of thing before. When Balaam recognized that the animal was right, the angel that the beast could see the entire time made its presence know to Balaam as well."

"Great, now we've got angels too." Harkin droned.

"This snide commentary of you is rather unbecoming of you, young man." Benji reprimanded.

"Sorry," Harkin relented, "tell me about the angel."

Benji smirked, "The angel told Balaam that had the beast not turned from the course those three times, then the angel would have killed Balaam. The angel was there to stand against Balaam because although God had told him to go, Balaam had not realized what God intended for him to do."

"Wait," Harkin interrupted, "this isn't part of a snide remark, but are you saying God was going to have the guy killed for doing what God told him to do in the first place?"

"Not exactly. Remember, God always has the full plan. I think He intended this intervention from the beginning. I imagine that is a word you are rather familiar with as well. So, why else let the beast see the angel first?"

"Fair point." Harkin conceded.

"I believe that although Balaam set out ready to fulfill what he thought was God's purpose, he had the wrong intent in his heart. Balaam was being paid and called on by a king to curse a people God intended to bless. So, when God sent an angel to intervene, it still took Balaam multiple opportunities to realize that it was even by God's design. He was just getting mad that things were going wrong."

"Is this your polite, preacherly way of telling me to stop getting upset because I'm the one screwing things up?" Harkin asked with a smirk.

Benji laughed before replying, "Maybe not in those words. More like, I'm trying to tell you instead of trying to fix what you think is going wrong, maybe you should be looking around to see if God is trying to intervene."

Harkin was silent and unwilling to be meet Benji's eyes. He let his wander out over the cemetery beside the little church, and for the first time, Harkin let himself take it all in. He had come here more times than he could count and more times than he would have wanted to, but he had never really paid attention to just how much work Benji did. The grass was not just cut or mowed. It was manicured and immaculate all the way down to the soft way it hugged the base of each headstone. For all the times that Harkin had walked in on it, this was the first time that he noticed that the gravel walkway was pristinely raked. In the foreboding field of green that hosted the shades of white and grey with the occasional black was still neatly nestled boutiques of various colors that even from this distance Harkin could tell were arranged all by the same person after being wind disheveled.

"I never realized how beautiful it is here." Harkin admitted.

"I know, but you're evading now." Benji replied.

"I don't know how to respond. Do you want me to believe that God wanted this to happen?" Harkin asked.

"Would that be so bad?" Benji challenged before continuing, "Look where it has brought you. You've made a friend other than a gravedigger."

Harkin shot the old man a withering frown when he saw Benji smirk.

Benji held a hand placatingly before continuing, "Sorry, it couldn't be avoided, but seriously. You have let go of some of your past. Finally, laying your sister to rest. You may not have forgiven your old man yet, but I don't think you hate him anymore. You are willing to try to rebuild a relationship with your mother. All of this while trying to help another young woman fight addiction and her own past. Even when she seems to have lost a battle, here you are, asking me how you can continue to help her. Maybe the beast that kept pulling you off course has finally asked you why you keep getting angry, and just maybe the angel that has been ready to just kill what was left of you is finally going to let you pass. Maybe you're ready to stop trying to curse everything and just be and receive a blessing."

"You think it's that easy?" Harkin asked.

"Oh, I never said it was easy," Benji corrected in a warm and soothing voice, "but you'll be glad you did the work nonetheless."

"All the times that you tried to preach to me and I told you that I didn't want to hear it. Were you hoping something like this would happen?" Harkin questioned.

"This seems like a horrible thing to hope for, but I suppose it is only fair that I admit that yes, I prayed your eyes would be opened." Benji answered.

"And was this an answer to your prayers?"

"I am hoping so," Benji said somberly, "only time will tell, but I have faith."

When Harkin only shook his head, Benji said, "And I even have faith for you until you're ready to have your own."

"I imagine there is no use in arguing and telling you that's not necessary, so how about for once I just say I appreciate it?"

"That would be a nice change of pace." Benji confirmed.

"Then let's just pretend I did that." Harkin said with a smile.

***

To My Unkindled Love,

At this point, in your change and recovery, you should feel encouraged to continue to increase your reliance on God as your source of guidance and as your strength to walk according to this guidance. By now, you should understand that part of you that you had to overcome, and you should understand that it was by a grace greater than you that you have overcome it thus far. You must remain vigilant not to forget that.

"May the words of my mouth and the meditations of my heart be pleasing to You, O Lord, my rock and my redeemer." (Psalm 19:14 NLT)

To continue your progress, you need to seek through prayer and mediation to improve your conscious contact with God as you understand Him, praying only for knowledge of His Will for you and the power to carry that out.

Understand the importance of this part of your recovery. The strength and power of God that allowed you to face yourself and overcome that part of yourself that would eventually destroy you is not a band-aid or surgery to a healing wound. You have entered into a relationship that will forever change you as long as you do not forsake that.

Evermore,
Your Kindred Heart

Chapter Twelve

To whom it May Concern;

Do you know the most depressing thing about a runner's high? The finish line. It does not matter whether it's winning the race or a loss, but the finish line means the race is over. You have to stop running and face the crash.

Nobody likes that the thought of that, just so you know, my dear friend. The subject of so many moral stories; what goes up must come down, and it all goes around. You don't get to enjoy that level of freedom without a price. That price is watching it all come reeling into that final moment. No clear thoughts or fleeting sensation of letting go of all the burdens as you sprint on ahead but rather just that line in the dirt *marking where it comes back to you again. You, my dear friend, just get the finish line. The reality crashing back down. Congratulations!*

You ran a great race but don't worry, everyone has to stop running—even you. You cannot outrun the end of the race.

Evermore,

The Last Race

✹✹✹

When Harkin came to visit the next day, he found Emily already sitting at the table as if she were anticipating him. She smiled when she saw him come in and gestured to the other chair. He noticed that the shine of her blue eyes was still a little dull, but she looked well. As he sat, he realized that she had draped his suit jacket, that he had apparently forgotten the day before, over the back of the chair.

"You forgot it," She said, noticing the way his eyes lingered, "and I'm sorry."

"For what?" Harkin asked, confused.

She held up an envelope with his name on it, "This was in the pocket. Have you read it?"

Harkin shook his head in response.

"Were you going to?" Emily pressed.

"I hadn't decided. Then, I forgot about it." Harkin admitted.

Emily nodded, "I read it last night, and I think you need to know what it says." She stopped to study his face, the expressionless eyes, and set of his jaw, "I would give it back to you if I thought you would read it for yourself. Instead, will you listen if I read it to you?"

For several minutes, they sat silently looking at one another until Harkin finally nodded.

"Okay," Harkin said, gesturing to the letter, "What did he have to say?"

Emily cleared her throat as she unfolded the letter, "My dear Harry, if you're reading this and I hope that my death will allow you to let go of enough of your hatred that you will read this, then it is time for you to know the truth."

As Emily paused to take a breath, she saw Harkin sit forward in his chair with a quizzical expression on his face. She hoped that was a good sign. She had spent most of the night trying to anticipate how he might react before realizing that she still had no idea how that might be. Before realizing that she did not know him well enough to anticipate anything but wishing that she did. She still wished she knew him better, even as she took a deep breath to keep reading his father's letter.

"I know you always blamed me for what happened to your sister, but I never had the heart to tell you that accidents happen. Whether it's fate or faith, I don't know, but sometimes they do happen. The day that car hit us," Emily wiped her eyes as she kept reading, "I was sober. You should know that. In fact, it wasn't a bar that I had come from that day but a meeting. I was going to show you all that night, and we were going to celebrate, but rather it became part of one of my best-kept secrets. I want you to have it for what little it's worth."

Emily slid a red coin across the table to Harkin, saying, "That was in the envelope with the letter. It's a sobriety chip. Not every group gives them out anymore, but among AA and a few NA groups, they still do celebrate that."

Harkin picked it up off the table, examining it in disbelief. Stamped in the middle of the emblem was one month, and along the edge, it read 'To Thine Own Self Be True.'

He tore his eyes from it to meet hers for the first time since she had started reading, then asked, "Do you have one of these?"

She shook her head before answering, "No, the clinic doesn't really do that anymore. It's mostly with individual support groups run outside of a fully-funded facility."

"Oh." Harkin said numbly.

"Can I keep reading?" She asked hesitantly. Emily waited while Harkin looked at the coin again, then she began reading again, "I was sober when I picked your sister up, and I had been for a month. I was going to turn my life around and do right by your mother and you kids. I stayed sober while Nora was alive, but the day we laid her in the ground...that was the last day I was sober. I know you and your mother paid for that, and I regret that. No, I don't ask for your forgiveness here because I should have been man enough to earn it before my last breath."

Harkin sat the chip on the table and made to stand up, but Emily spoke in an eerily calm voice that stopped him, "There's more."

"I've heard enough, really." He insisted.

"Sit down. I'm not done." Her calm did not break, but there was a fire in it that Harkin obeyed. She cleared her throat, and her eyes scanned for where she left off, "But son, if there is anything I can leave you with, let it be this. I pray for you. I truly do. I don't know how this letter will come into your hands, but if you don't know already, your mother had been dragging me to church. The pastor there says he sees you from time to time, and I'm glad for that, but I cannot help but think you haven't seen the fire he can preach with."

Emily stopped, and Harkin realized he was smiling at his father's mention of Benji. When he noticed her watching him, he motioned for her to keep reading, so she did with a small smile of her own.

"There's one story he likes to bring up about a group of lepers and a city under siege. He has all kinds of messages that he ties into it, but I won't test your patience by going through them all. What I want to tell you has to do with the story that Pastor Ben doesn't talk much about. The man who was trampled at the gate. He could not believe that such miracles could happen as what the prophet told him, and when it became a reality, the king sent him to restrict access to the miracle, so to speak. The man died within sight of a blessing because he did not believe. Son, don't let what I've done or the way that I've lived only let you get close enough to die within sight of something better. Believe that blessings can happen. Don't make my mistakes. Love, Dad."

Emily folded the letter back before sliding into the envelope and placing it onto the table in front of Harkin. The entire time, she was aware of the heavy silence. When she finally looked up at him, she saw the same expressionless eyes and features that he had worn so often, and another part of her wanted to cry. If he saw it in her face, he did not say it. Harkin dropped his eyes to the letter on the table but made no move to pick it up.

"I'm sorry." She repeated.

Harkin seemed to shrug it off, "You don't need to apologize."

"Yes, I do. I am apologizing now that I know what happened and," She paused to take a deep breath, "for what I need to say next."

Harkin's expressionless eyes showed a new curiosity, but he did not say anything, so she continued.

"If you couldn't ever forgive him for something that wasn't even his fault, how can you not hate me? Someone is dead because of me. Two junkies took the life of a kid who was going to do great things in this world." She said as the tears filled her eyes again.

This time she felt seared by the cold intensity that returned to his eyes. For the longest time, he didn't say anything. Under his gaze, she realized it was probably only a few seconds, but it felt as if eternity had passed under that harsh chill.

When he finally spoke, his voice held all the warmth needed to melt that wicked freeze, "How can you ask me that? You're not the only one in this room who feels responsible for the death of someone." Harkin slid the letter back toward Emily, "Do you need to read that again? I killed him. At the very least, I drove him right back to the thing that he had overcome. Right back to the thing that killed him in the end. I cursed a man who was looking for a blessing."

"That's not true-" Emily started.

"I already failed one addict. I'm not doing that again." Harkin interrupted with his conviction.

"You can't put what I've done on you. That's not fair, it's not right, it's not true, and it's not healthy for either of us." She said, matching his conviction.

"You were right." Harkin admitted.

"You're going to have to be more specific." She teased.

"Stars and islands. That's what we are to each other. We led each other into the storms, but we will be there to pick up all the broken pieces too."

Emily smiled and ran a finger along the edge of Eugene's letter, "Believe in blessings and don't let each other die with them only insight?"

"Something like that." Harkin agreed with a smile.

"So, what do we do now?" She asked cautiously.

"I'm not pushing you." Harkin answered.

"I know." She replied, "But again, what if you didn't have to push?"

"Then I guess I would have to ask, what do you want? If you say you want this, then what is *this*?" Harkin pressed.

"And, if I didn't know?" Emily pursued nervously.

"I don't have to go anywhere. I can give you the time to find out. In fact, you will have plenty of time to find out."

She raised an eyebrow to him as she asked, "What does that mean? I will have plenty of time."

"Once you leave this clinic, you will resume your counseling with Ray, and it will not be healthy for you to have a relationship for what was it a year. So, you will have plenty of time to figure out what you want."

"So, it can't be a relationship?" She pressed with a wounded note in her voice.

"Not for a while, but there is nothing saying we can't be friends." Harkin said with a shrug and a smile.

"I'd like that." Emily replied, her lips turning up to a soft, nervous smile in return.

"But don't think I've forgotten." He said tauntingly.

"Forgotten what?" She asked with an uneasiness entering her blue eyes.

"This qualifies as another time, doesn't it? What to tell me about your letters?" Harkin asked.

"Oh," She said, her features turning crestfallen, "I really had hoped you would forget. But I guess I do owe you that much."

"You don't owe me anything. If you really don't want to, I understand." Harkin interrupted.

She gave him a disapproving scowl before she said, "Stop doing that. Stop giving me an out. If I say, I owe you, then let me decide that and make any retribution I see fit."

Harkin held up his hands defensively, "Sorry."

She sighed discontentedly, "It's fine, but don't do it again. Now, do you want to know or not?"

"Yes."

"Okay," Emily began with a deep exhalation, "The letters like I said last time are a way to track progress. Mostly mental and emotional progress. When Ray checked me in again, he brought that notebook back. It was the one that I had started the last time."

She paused, trying to find the words to continue, and Harkin waited patiently. She found herself looking into his eyes, and for the first time, she could see more than just the empty chill. She felt the warmth of the deep brown eyes pouring into her, and she felt it strengthening her. She had not looked so deeply into his eyes until this moment, or maybe she had, but she had not been in the position to need the warmth like she did right now. She had thought she was doing okay until she was not, but now sitting in the clinic having relapsed and having made that mistake again, she was looking at a man that, for all of his mistakes, still radiated encouragement for her.

"The early letters were addressed to no one specifically. They were more ranting as I came off the withdrawal and crash, then began to overcome the urge to just want to get high again. Ray visited me a lot that first time and counseled me individually from a biblical perspective on top of the mandatory counseling that the clinic requires. That was when the shift in the letters started."

"To my unkindled love from your kindred heart?" Harkin asked.

"Yes."

"What does that mean?" He pressed.

She looked away from him with an embarrassed smile, "Okay, this is just mortifying."

"You don't-" Harkin trailed off at the scornful look she fixed him with, "okay, okay. Finish the story. Humiliations and all."

Emily stuck her tongue out at him before saying, "Just because I told you to stop being so sincerely supporting doesn't mean you need to be so sarcastic. Love your neighbor as yourself."

"We're friends, not neighbors." Harkin stated.

"No, that's not what I meant. I was trying to explain. It's from the Bible." She stopped at the smirk on Harkin's face, "You were messing with me, weren't you?"

He winked at her, "Maybe just a little. You did just call me sarcastic."

"Well, you basically just said you loved me." Emily shot back.

"So, I wasn't completely insincere." Harkin returned. Emily's mouth fell open in surprise, but she did not say anything, so Harkin continued,

"Love your neighbor as yourself. How does that explain the letters?"

Emily nodded, accepting the change in subject, "Ray had talked about that verse one day, but the thing he didn't understand was in order to follow that verse, you have to love yourself in order to love your neighbor. I had to learn to do that again. I told you I lost a son?"

"Spencer." Harkin answered.

"Yes, losing him broke my heart. I spent the time carrying him, preparing to love him. Then when he was born, I started to pour that love out, so when he died, all of that love just died too. This probably sounds so pitiful."

"No, go on." Harkin pressed.

"Ray started helping process that grief, and I realized that I needed to find that love again. I still love my son, but I need to turn some of that love back toward me. My unkindled love."

"From your kindred heart. You meant from your broken heart, didn't you?"

"Kindred. With God, we all have in common that we are broken people. We all have contrite hearts. You've just gotten to read parts of mine."

"And you'll get to know mine. If that's what you want."

"I'd like that." She said with a nervous smile.

※※※

To My Unkindled Love,

Now is when your real journey begins. By now, you should know that feeling of hope burning inside of you again. You must be willing to be the harbinger of hope to those who still feel lost in hopelessness.

Having been renewed in yourself through your own spiritual pathway and having found genuine hope in being able to stay clean and recover, you must now aim to both continue this pathway of change, yourself, and also share your journey and hope with others.

"Dear brothers and sisters, if another believer is overcome by some sin, you who are Godly should gently and humbly help that person back on to the right path. And be careful not to fall into the same temptation yourself." (Galatians 6:1NLT)

Some call it witnessing or evangelism, but you remain only a harbinger of hope. Having experienced a spiritual awakening, you must try to carry this same message of change and recovery and the ability to have the strength to overcome you to others in need of the same abilities not just in your words but by the practicing of these principles in all of your affairs.

Evermore,

Your Kindred Heart

Darren Finney

Epilogue

Harkin pressed record on his phone from the back of the church. He had talked to the prison therapist who had approved it, and he had agreed to record this for Misty, much to Emily's chagrin. Harkin had a hard time focusing on his phone. He had to admit as beautiful as she looked, even despite his self-insistence that he would not let any relationship between them progress beyond a friendship until after the first year of her recovery this time.

Emily was standing behind the pulpit of the church in a floor-length, round-neck, short sleeve maxi dress that Rosie had gotten for her. Again, it was another dress that Rosie had felt the solid teal color would better accentuate her blue eyes. Emily loved it because it was comfortable. She was not as worried as

Rosie about drawing everyone's attention to her eyes, especially now that she knew their true-blue color was still a little tarnished as she worked to remain clean again. As she thought about the dress, Emily took a deep breath and looked over her shoulder where Rosie stood supportively and stoically. After Harkin had told her about the Scotts' son, she had wanted to speak to Ray, and with his blessing, she told Rosie the entire story. She had not expected Rosie to be willing to support her again, much less be willing to forgive her. However, Emily was surprised to learn that Rosie had made an effort to reach out to Misty as well in an attempt to offer her the same loving support that she had so far showed Emily. Emily wondered how much of that Ray had a hand in.

It was Rosie, Emily realized, who had first offered up this idea for Emily to give her testimony in front of the church, to give her a chance to place every detail of her story in front of everyone so that she would not have to live in fear of them anymore. It was also Rosie, and Emily was unfathomably thankful for her, who offered to stand with Emily up here while she spoke.

"Anytime you're ready, dear." Rosie's soft voice whispered behind her.

Emily took another deep breath and offered Rosie a nervous smile, wondering now if she should have had Rosie, Ray, or even Harkin read over what she was about to say, "I may have done this, but I'm not as bad as that person. I would not have done what that person did. I will never be as bad as that person. I will never be that person again. That person is our biggest failure. That person is our worst secret. Satan loves to remind us about that person."

Emily looked up from her paper she had laid on the pulpit in front of her to scan the church, biting nervously on her bottom lip before she continued, "You can feel free to substitute guy, moron, woman, girl, or whatever suits you best because if we're honest and open with ourselves, we all have a 'that person' in our past or present or just somewhere in us that we carry. I know for certain I do anyway, and I carry her around every day because I just can't seem to lay her to rest."

Rosie placed a hand on her shoulder, and Emily reached up to squeeze it. From where he was sitting, Harkin could visibly see the tremor in Emily as she steeled herself to keep going.

"So today, I am hoping that by sharing her with you, I can finally make some peace with her. For me, that person sought refuge in drugs and substances to dull the pain and give me a false sense of happiness. I thought I had it all under control. At first, I told myself I needed them because I was in pain." A bitter chuckle escaped Emily as she continued, "It seemed justifiable, and the voice in my head always had an excuse. When I started taking stronger drugs, it seemed logical to believe that it was necessary because I was only building a tolerance. The problem was I could feel the effects of the drugs that were supposed to be the warning signs; a dense mental fog, constant drowsiness, always unaware, and just large gaps of time that I don't remember like how I got to the hospital the first time or the four months leading up to that overdose, but it was okay because I was not as bad as that person."

Emily's eyes swept the church again, and Harkin could see the tears gleaming on her cheeks. Her eyes lingered on him with a sad smile on her lips, and for a moment, she kept her eyes on him as she started speaking again, "In this case, it was that person with a serious drug problem because mine wasn't a problem. I had gotten help for mine, not by choice, but that didn't matter because as long as I had gotten help, I could fool myself into believing that I wasn't that person. I could fool myself into thinking that I could handle life without returning to all of my bad habits. That I could deal healthily. I could fool myself into thinking I wasn't that person until I was faced with everything that I had been trying to bury in that fog. The death of my infant son, the choices I had made, and that it was my fault that my best friend was in prison." At this, Emily turned to look at Rosie, "That it was because of me that your son was killed."

Emily turned back to the congregation gathered that morning that had now fallen into a discomforting quiet. Harkin saw the strength in her eyes this time, and he wondered if that hush and somehow encouraged her.

"Raymond Scott Junior was killed when my best friend left me at the curb of the hospital when I had overdosed and sped away because she was afraid of being caught high. She would not have been on the road that night had it not been for the person I had become. He was killed for the person that I was still trying to hide. That's why I need to tell you today..."

Emily trailed off, and Harkin felt his chest tighten in anxiety for her. Apparently, Rosie felt something similar because she had stepped closer to Emily, but Emily waved her off, blinking away new tears.

"I need to tell you today that when we become that person, we hit rock bottom, and we hit it hard. And... it is a lie to think that it just makes it all that much easier to look up. No, by the time we hit that ultimate low, we are too ashamed, too embarrassed, or too remorseful to truly lookup. But I have some small comfort for you today." Emily said with a smile that torn Harkin to pieces and left tears in his eyes, "Christ has been dealing with that person from the beginning. In fact, that person got a pass so that Jesus could be beaten then nailed to a cross." Emily looked back down at what she had written, not to gather strength but to make sure that she could remember all the notes she had made from Ray's visits to her this last time in the clinic, "Matthew 27, Mark 15, John 18, and Luke 23 all deal with the release of Barabbas. A convicted criminal, murderer, and insurrectionist. The last person that should have been set free. That never deserved that chance. The person that compared to who took his place could never have earned that mercy, but God had bigger plans. Barabbas, the Biblical equivalent of the modern-day 'that person,' got away clean because Jesus had to die for our sin. Jesus had to die and be resurrected to bring us salvation and eternal life."

"Amen." Pastor Ray said from where he had been sitting on the front pew.

The momentary interruption and encouragement seemed to cause Emily to lose her momentum and falter for a brief instant, earning Ray a quick scowl from his wife behind Emily. Harkin smiled briefly at that, glad to know for once he was not the one earning that disapproving look.

Pulling back into her composure, Emily smiled at Ray and pressed on, "The world called for the release of Barabbas. I'm sure you guys knew that, but I didn't. The world will choose that person every time. It's important for me to talk about that. Satan's most powerful weapon and this earthly world's greatest ally is that person. Do you know why? That person is so detrimental to our spiritual health and well-being as well as our relationship with Christ because we cannot lay that person to rest. We hold on to the shame, the hurt, and the regret. Those feelings damage us because we, in all that pain, cannot feel love. That person that we carry in the back of our minds that makes us so ashamed of ourselves makes love impossible. I am going to repeat this a third time because I really want you to understand this today." Emily said in a voice that held all of her stern resolve, "If you don't walk away with anything else but a bad opinion of me after today, please remember this. Left to their own devices in this world, that person makes love impossible. Satan uses that person to fill our heads in the worst of times with thoughts like; no one can ever truly love me; God could never use somebody like me. I'm not worth their love. I'm not worth God's love. Do these thoughts sound familiar to anyone else? How about these?

I don't deserve them. I could never have that. I'm not worthy of His grace."

Harkin felt the soul-searing gaze of those too blue eyes as they swept over him to meet every eye in the sanctuary before she continued.

"All these thoughts pull us deeper into this world, into our sin. All these thoughts tear at us until we are not just heart-broken... but completely broken. They tear at us until we deny ourselves the experience of love. We start believing the thoughts, the lies. We begin to doubt that our spouses really love us, we worry that our kids will never truly understand what it means to be family, we give up on the hope that we are loved by God, and we start looking for something to replace that love with. All of this because we will not just lay that person to rest in God's love.

That person that you think nobody else can love is who God wanted to love. And I don't know if anyone else needed to know that today, but it was what I needed to know for a very long time."

Emily finished with a fresh wave of tears as she turned to wrap Rosie in a hug, who had been silently crying as well. As the two women stood there holding each other in that embrace, the church applauded.